Alternative Ways

(Paperback Edition)

A Novel
By
Victor Ralph

Grosvenor House
Publishing Limited

All rights reserved
Copyright © Victor Ralph, 2024

The right of Victor Ralph to be identified as the author of this work has been asserted in accordance with Section 78 of the Copyright, Designs and Patents Act 1988

The book cover is copyright to Victor Ralph

This book is published by
Grosvenor House Publishing Ltd
Link House
140 The Broadway, Tolworth, Surrey, KT6 7HT.
www.grosvenorhousepublishing.co.uk

This book is sold subject to the conditions that it shall not, by way of trade or otherwise, be lent, resold, hired out or otherwise circulated without the author's or publisher's prior consent in any form of binding or cover other than that in which it is published and without a similar condition including this condition being imposed on the subsequent purchaser.

This book is a work of fiction. Any resemblance to people or events, past or present, is purely coincidental.

A CIP record for this book
is available from the British Library

ISBN 978-1-83615-002-2

Contents

Acknowledgements	v
Prologue	vii
Chapter 1	1
Chapter 2	9
Chapter 3	15
Chapter 4	23
Chapter 5	31
Chapter 6	39
Chapter 7	45
Chapter 8	55
Chapter 9	61
Chapter 10	73
Chapter 11	79
Chapter 12	85
Chapter 13	93
Chapter 14	103
Chapter 15	111
Chapter 16	119
Chapter 17	125
Chapter 18	135
Chapter 19	143
Chapter 20	151

Chapter 21	157
Chapter 22	167
Chapter 23	175
Chapter 24	181
Chapter 25	185
Chapter 26	193
About the Author	195

Acknowledgments

Any research that I have needed for the book has been mainly carried out online so I guess my thanks must go to the World Wide Web for making it happen.

Thanks also to those friends who I have persuaded to read a chapter or two and whose feedback and encouragement has been the motivation for me to keep writing.

However, my real thanks must go to my wife Teresa who, with pencil at the ready, has read and re-read the manuscript pointing out my errors and making helpful suggestions that have ensured that the novel has been greatly improved.

Prologue

Coming from a family that spent more money on drink, cigarettes and betting on the greyhounds than on food meant that, as a boy, Andy Clewer was always hungry. Not much money was spent on clothes either. His trousers, shirts and jackets were mostly too big for him, came from charity shops or were hand me downs from friends and family.

The youngest of four boys with the street his playground life was tough. Tooting High Road secondary school was a nightmare of bullying and humiliation for young Andy. Made fun of as an undernourished skinny urchin he had few mates and was always in trouble with his teachers.

When others did well, they got praise but with Andy it was different.

'Have you copied this work from someone Clewer?' Mr Barwell his teacher had a sadistic streak and would boom out from the front of the classroom. 'You've even got some of it right.'

The rest of the class would snigger. At break time he would be teased. 'Got something right Clewer, pity your trousers don't fit.' They would laugh and push him, form a circle and jeer at him. It took all his effort and a face screwed up tight to fight back the tears.

In later life he could smile as he recalled the words that the teacher had spoken to him on the day he left.

'You've wasted my time trying to teach you. Perhaps Borstal will have more luck because that's where you'll end up. You, Clewer, will never amount to anything.'

'Well, eat your words Mister smart arse Barwell.' He thought. 'Cos look at me now. I'm the richest kid that ever went to that school. I've got my own multi-million-pound business and I make more money in a year than you'll earn in your lifetime.'

But he hadn't forgotten how it felt to be a poor kid with nothing much to look forward to. With business on the up Andy had invested in a run-down warehouse that he had converted into a youth club with a small café, snooker and table tennis tables, a stereo system a small dance floor and a seating area. It was a place where kids could go, be safe and have some fun and a sense of purpose. Whenever he could Andy would visit, play a couple of games of snooker and tell the youngsters how he lived just down the road and started life like them. He explained how anyone could get on if they tried hard enough and could be just like him, a successful businessman. It gave him a kick to be able to help lift the spirits of the young people who probably felt like he had once.

But tonight, it was all about a totally different environment and a different way of life.

Chapter 1

Andy Clewer was eager to ensure that the evening's dinner party was a success. The guests were key customers of his company, Clewer Alternatives and the evening was organised so that he could impress the influential guests in an attempt to get them to buy more of his products.

The company produced and manufactured herbal and natural remedies and was growing in size as it expanded its customer base. Tonight's guests could pave the way to a significant step up in sales and Andy was wanting to be at his sparkling best. As it happened, he got much more than sales out of the evening, a liaison that would start a chain of events of which he would have never dreamt.

He had booked a private dining room at the Michelin starred Bridgedale, an exclusive and expensive restaurant on the banks of the Thames. The plan was to arrive by boat and have the guests greeted personally by the Chef Patron Jacques Rowle.

The boat, a cabin cruiser almost forty feet long, glided up to the landing stage and the crew of two girls jumped off and pulled on mooring lines to expertly secure the boat. Andy stepped confidently from the still rocking boat onto the landing stage and turned to his guests.

"Let me introduce you to my friend Jacques who has assured me that he will be supervising the kitchens personally tonight."

As they disembarked, the guests and Andy's wife Suzanne, were helped onto dry land by Jacques Rowle himself. The men were resplendent in black dinner jackets, the ladies in cocktail dresses that had designer label written all over them. The one exception was Andy himself who wore a white tuxedo that made him the natural focal point of interest. Not that he needed any introductions. His face often appeared in newspapers and on television news as the owner and chief executive of the largest provider of alternative medicine products in Europe. This was a company that was rapidly growing under Andy's determined and aggressive drive.

They were shown through to their private dining room by Jacques who, after making his apologies, left them to oversee the kitchen.

"Good evening, Mr Clewer," said Jean Paul the maître d', knowing that good service and deference to a guest like Andy Clewer would bring a sizeable tip, usually in the region of a couple of hundred pounds or more.

A discreet bar in one corner was there to provide pre-dinner cocktails with guests being greeted with the driest of dry martinis, a stuffed cocktail olive drowning in the potent liquid. The small group chatted as they nibbled at a selection of canapés, waiters ensuring that any empty martini glasses were swapped with freshly filled replacements. It had not gone unnoticed by Suzanne that her husband was paying close attention to the expanse of chest displayed by the Vincent Floyd's young wife Miriam.

The principal guests were all from the retail industry and the intention this evening was to forge a bond between the lucrative 'over the counter' drugs market and his own, smaller market, of natural remedies so as to increase sales.

George Nicol together with his wife Annie owned and operated a chain of convenience stores which traded under the banner of Any Time and were a feature of many a housing estate and small town in most counties of England and Wales. The shops were open from early morning until late at night seven days a week and were the mainstay of people who need to pop to the shops for those forgotten items.

Then there was Henry Lord and his long-time partner Tara. Henry was Purchasing Director of Buyrite Supermarkets the country's third largest retailer with sales in excess of £4 billion and with more than 75,000 employees. Buyrite featured pharmacies in many of their stores and Andy was already in discussion with Henry on a range of natural remedies being stocked in stores in London and the Southeast of England.

As if conducting an orchestra Andy arranged his guests round the table.

"Suzanne, you sit at that end of the table Vincent, next to me, I need to talk to you and perhaps Miriam on my other side. George you and Henry can sit either side of Suzanne and Annie and Tara can fit in between."

Within a few minutes he had set the scene just as he wanted and he looked down the table toward his wife.

Suzanne still had the stunning beauty that had caught Andy's attention when they first met at the races in Newbury some twelve years ago but the once shapely figure was now a size sixteen pushing eighteen. Try as she might, losing a stone and a dress size was beyond her reach as she thought but as Andy liked to say, beyond her willpower.

The meal was to start with a smoked chicken and mango salad, followed by seared scallops and then roast loin of wild venison in a berry sauce as the main course. The wines to accompany the meal had been entrusted to the Sommelier at the Bridgedale, a wine expert with an impeccable taste and knowledge when it came to matching wine and food.

"Well Andy what's so important that you need me next to you?" Vincent sat back as a waiter unfolded his napkin and with a flourish deposited it neatly over his lap.

He glanced across the table at his wife Miriam who at thirty years of age was almost twenty five years younger than her husband. Vincent was the Chairman and major shareholder in Floyds Chemists, the largest independent high street chemists in the country. With more than three hundred shops throughout mainland Britain, they also had shops in the Channel Islands and Gibraltar. In fact any English tourist who visited the Rock found comfort in the familiar logo and layout of Floyds on Gibraltar's Main Street, where it stood next to that other quintessential bastion of the UK, Marks and Spencer. He met Andy's gaze full on.

"I want to talk to you about taking on some extra products from our Way of Life range. Not everyone wants to stuff themselves full of drugs containing heaven knows what and I believe there is room for expanding natural alternatives alongside the proprietary brands. The one I have in mind is a natural alternative to Viagra;" Andy winked. "Amongst other things, profits should go up as well."

"You mean that's what's called doing what comes naturally." Miriam gave a throaty chuckle. Her petite figure was shown to full advantage by the dress she had bought earlier in Paris, for just such an occasion. The carefully sculpted neckline, barely hidden beneath the bolero jacket, revealed tantalising glimpses of her full rounded breasts. Vincent laughed and gave his young wife a loving smile.

The starter appeared before the diners, delivered in silent unison by waiters who were directed by the wave of the white gloves of Jean Paul.

Miriam dipped her finger into the creamy dressing that adorned the salad. She turned her gaze on Andy as she ran her tongue down her finger, sucking the dressing into her mouth.

"M'mm this is heaven." She raised her eyes and smiled at Andy.

"So what is this wonder alternative to Viagra, one of your weird concoctions I have no doubt?" Vincent shot a quick look toward the other end of the table where Suzanne sat.

"You probably think I'm making this up but on my word, it's called Horny Goat Weed and it's grown in China. Apparently when goats had been grazing on the hillsides where it grows, they well, they became more amorous shall we say, than when grazing on other pastures, hence the name Horny Goat Weed." Andy grinned.

Vincent's glass was nearly empty and as he nodded his thanks to the Sommelier who added some more of the deliciously fruity white burgundy, he turned to Andy.

"Good heavens surely you don't market it under that name. I wouldn't know if I was in a chemist shop or a garden centre if I saw that on the shelf." He laughed lightly at his own joke.

The empty plates had been removed and their replacements were heaped with seared, caramelised scallops sitting on slivers of crisp leeks bathed in a balsamic and olive oil reduction.

Miriam had been enjoying their host's hospitality and having started the evening with several dry martinis was well into the burgundy.

"Well, you two are a couple of old goats. Which one of you is horny, is it you Andy?" She giggled.

It was at that moment that there was one of those sudden lulls in the conversation and Miriam's words carried the full length of the table.

"Whatever are you three talking about, you told me it would be all business but it sounds more like a proposition to me?" Suzanne quizzed angrily.

The two women eyed each other down the table.

"Darling," slurred Miriam, "are you a teensy bit jealous?" The air between the two women was filled with hostile rivalry.

"Come on you two, Vincent and I are talking about a product made from a plant called Horny Goat Weed that's all. Not that you'd know goats were horny unless, I suppose, you were another goat." Andy laughed as he tried to ease the tension.

Once again, the plates were cleared and a champagne flute full of citron sorbet was placed in front of each of the diners. The early autumn dusk was starting to fall and they could see the lights of boats as they passed out on the river. The mood had changed to one of friendly conviviality as they enjoyed the good food, wine and ambience of their surroundings.

"All this talk is making me thirsty, any chance of some red?" George Nicol leaned forward as he asked Andy. George was known to be somewhat partial to his drink and had on several occasions been discreetly removed from more than one famous eatery. "Horny Goat Weed, trust the Chinese to come up with something like that. No wonder the population of China is over a billion, I bet all the males are on the jolly old Horny Goat Weed."

"I'll put some counter displays in, what say 30 of your stores on sale or return. If you don't shift the stock in a month, you'll get your money back on the returns."

"Seems a good deal to me, I'll send you a list of sites where I think the customers might go for such a thing." George looked round as the Sommelier suggested that he might like to try the next wine, a weighty and full bodied 2011 Chateauneuf-Du-Pape, to accompany the venison. "Excellent, just what the doctor ordered." He said smacked his lips appreciatively. This was taken as the OK to serve the wine to the rest of the guests.

"How about you Henry, can I put counter displays in your stores with pharmacies?"

"Same deal as George, sale or return and you're on." Henry knew he couldn't go wrong with an arrangement like that.

Andy didn't like the way Miriam and Suzanne continued to face up to each other down the length of the table. He could feel that Miriam had slipped off her shoe and was rubbing her foot up and down the back of his leg under the table whilst at the same time, smiling at his wife.

"I can't believe Andy needs goat weed or any other weed to make him horny, come on Suzanne give us the low down we're all friends here."

"Don't you think Miriam might like some water to dilute all that wine she's been drinking?" Suzanne glared at her husband.

The tension between the two women was broken as the waiters appeared ready to serve the main course. The small talk started once again as gleaming white plates covered with silver domes were placed in front of each of them.

Glancing round and taking their cue from Jean Paul with a well-rehearsed flourish and in co-ordinated perfection, the domes were whisked from the top of the plates. Succulent slices of just pink venison were revealed layered on braised red cabbage, bolstered by the addition of quenelles of celeriac pureed with creamed horseradish.

The diners concentrated on enjoying the well flavoured meat, their glasses being refilled by the attentive Sommelier who made sure that no one went without.

Suzanne and Miriam's spate was forgotten as they each expressed their appreciation of Jacques Rowle's creation.

Andy had secured a promise from Vincent that he would get his secretary to talk with his to set up a meeting for the two of them to discuss a joint promotion of the Horny Goat Weed product in Floyds. He was certain that he could put together a deal that would see his new range featured in the majority of Floyds' branches.

The deal with Floyds and those with George Nicol and Henry Lord meant that the evening has been a huge success. These deals were not only lucrative to him and his company but such was his vanity and arrogance that Andy saw himself as bringing alternative medicines within the understanding and reach of those less opportune than himself.

He surveyed the table with satisfaction, not bad for a South London boy from a council estate. It gave him a sense of power that these rich and successful people were here at his behest, enjoying his hospitality. If only his old form teacher at the secondary modern school he'd attended could see him now. He felt good.

OK so he'd had a bit of bad luck backing the horses lately but he could soon turn that around. His best horse was due to run in some big races this season and he fancied himself in the winners' enclosure at Cheltenham. Business was on the up, his business that he'd started and built up from scratch, new products coming on stream what could go wrong?

It also felt good that Miriam was still stroking his leg with her foot. He looked down the table to his wife and smiled. Brian his chauffeur would be driving him and Suzanne home so he would enjoy a very large cognac with his coffee, yes life was good.

Chapter 2

It was two weeks after the dinner at the Bridgedale that Andy sat in his office at his company's headquarters in Surrey. Recently built, it was a modern office block of concrete, stainless steel and glass that occupied a prime position in the business park. It faced the man-made lake where, from its centre, a powerful jet of water sprayed high into the air. It cascaded down with a sound like falling rain onto the ducks and swans that swam around at a leisurely pace having made their homes on the reed covered banks. The tranquillity was only broken by the persistent hum of traffic on the adjacent M3 motorway.

That is until Andy opened the recorded delivery letter that Debbie, his secretary, had brought in with the rest of that morning's post. On the front in bold block capitals were the words 'Most Private & Confidential – for the Eyes of the Addressee Only'.

"Bloody hell;" he shouted, "they can't do that."

"Everything OK?" Debbie put her head through the door and looked at her Boss inquiringly.

"No, it bloody well isn't, I need to talk to...," he paused, "no it doesn't matter, just make sure that I'm not disturbed by anybody for the next half-hour."

She opened her mouth to remind him that he was to chair a meeting of the Development & Research Committee later that morning but Andy beat her to it.

"Anybody includes you and don't tell me about any meetings. They can bloody well wait as well." His fist banged down onto the desk with such force that the photo of Suzanne that always stood in a silver frame beside the slim line computer monitor fell over with a clatter.

Debbie retreated to her own office wondering what had put him into such a bad humour when earlier that morning he had been quite cheerful. He had told her how he was looking forward to going to see his horse run in a warm up race at Uttoxeter before going for the XYZ Steeplechase at Cheltenham.

"The prize to the winner is £28,000"' he had rubbed his hands together as he told her that, "not too shabby for jumping over a few fences." But that was before the letter arrived.

In his office Andy's thoughts were also on racing but in his case, it was the contents of the letter that was making him think - think and worry. It was there in black and white. 'You have 5 days in which to settle your considerably overdue betting account', it said. 'Failing which you leave us with no alternative but to seek recourse through the courts or to take whatsoever other steps we deem necessary to recover any monies outstanding. This may include having you declared bankrupt'. He stared, eyes gazing blankly at the words on the paper, lost in a turmoil of thoughts and desperation.

The phone rang. Striding across the office Andy flung open the door with such force that it crashed back against the wall and bounced back toward him.

"Don't you understand plain English you stupid bitch, I said no interruptions."

"It's a Mr Salmon. He said it was urgent and that you'd want to talk with him if you had received his recorded delivery letter. I knew you'd got the letter, so I assumed;" her voice faltered as Andy stood there glaring at her. Debbie's lip quivered. She had never seen Andy so aggressive and he had certainly never spoken to her in that way before.

"Well, what are you waiting for, put him through." The door slammed shut as he made his way back to his desk.

Mike Salmon was one of the Personal Account Managers that Leisure Industries assigned to their major account holders. Leisure Industries operated betting exchanges where you could bet on almost anything anywhere in the world. This was no high street bookmaker that took one pound each way bets but an organisation where bets of five, ten or even twenty thousand pounds a time were not uncommon. Much of this type of betting was carried out online. They also operated as a normal bookmaker where clients could place bets by phone.

Composing himself Andy picked up the phone. "Mike, I was going to call you later today, get a few meetings out of the way first then suggest we meet for lunch."

"I'd rather talk about your account now Andy, your secretary says that you've got our letter. Even with someone of your standing we get concerned when they've overstepped their limit and then miss the payment date;" Mike paused, "again and I'm under pressure from above to get things sorted."

"No problem;" Andy thought fast, I could put a cheque in the post today; you'd get it by tomorrow or the next day at the latest."

"Why not arrange a BACS transfer, quick and easy and we would have the money today, your account would be in order and with Cheltenham coming up you could enjoy your racing and perhaps win some of that money back."

He felt the phone slipping against his ear. Taking a handkerchief from his pocket Andy wiped the sweat from his face.

"Of course, I didn't think of that, I'll organise it straight away." His voice carried a confidence that he didn't feel. There was of course, no way that he could let on that his bank had already spoken to him about the overdraft that was running close to fifty thousand pounds and which he was being urged to reduce.

"Good show let's save the lunch for some other time. Andy, I've got to tell you that your credit limit has been reduced to five thousand ponds with immediate effect, at least that is, until you can convince the powers that be that you can settle your account on time. Sorry but that's the way it is. See you at Cheltenham." Mike rang off.

"Yes," said Andy to himself, "see you at Cheltenham."

He sat there lost in thought. How had he managed to get himself so much into debt? It didn't occur to him that he overlooked his losing bets whilst bragging about his wins. His view that he'd worked hard so why shouldn't he splash out on the good things in life meant that his outgoings nearly always exceeded his income. The thing was what he was going to do about it?

Settling his betting account was a simple task if he didn't stop to think of the implications of taking money that belonged to the Company. Well, it was his Company after all. Turning to the computer that was networked into the Company mainframe he keyed in his password. The screen came to life as he selected accounts from the option menu displayed in front of him.

He scrolled down until he reached the heading Marketing and Advertising and again, using a password unique to himself, accessed the programme that controlled the movement of the marketing funds that were available. Unlocking a drawer in his desk he pulled out a folder that contained the monthly statements of his betting account. Pausing only to check the sort code and account number of Leisure Industries bank account he transferred forty-two thousand pounds, giving his own betting account number as a reference.

He couldn't risk taking any more money from the Marketing Account, so he'd have to settle his overdraft with one big bet. If only it was a bet that he knew he'd win, then all his money problems would be over. He stood up and walked across to the window. God, he thought to himself, I could do with cheering up right now.

Turning back to his desk he leaned over, picked up the phone and dialled a number he'd committed to memory. "Hello, it's me are you doing anything this afternoon?" A smile spread across his face.

"That sounds outrageous, chocolate paint for me to lick off?" He listened again. "I'm on my way, usual place, just make sure you're ready." Picking up his mobile phone he dialled the number of a hotel by the river in Egham and booked a room, for the rest of the day. Opening the door to Debbie's office he was still smiling.

"I'm going out now. I may be back later if not I'll see you in the morning. Vincent Floyd is coming in tomorrow to negotiate terms on the Way of Life range, make sure that all the figures are on my desk and I'll get in early to go through them with Don."

Don Markham was Finance Director and was the one who put together pricing strategies for all of their major customers. He had been with Clewer Alternatives virtually since Andy had set up the business and was the financial brain that looked after the bottom line. In fact, Don was constantly arguing with Andy over his extravagant expenditure. He had nearly gone ballistic when he had seen Andy's expense claim with the receipts from the Bridgedale. The evening had cost more than three and a half thousand pounds. What with the restaurant bill of nearly two thousand, the overtime for the two girls on the boat, not to mention the cost of the chauffeur driven cars to take everyone home after the meal, it had put a hefty dent in the month's entertaining budget.

"Get off early why don't you Debbie. Anyone wants to know where I am say, oh, say I'm with the bank." Andy, his spirits lifted, felt generous and with that he was gone leaving Debbie open mouthed at the change of her Boss's mood.

The affair had started by pure chance. Oh yes, he knew that Miriam had been flirting with him at the Bridgedale and that he'd played along with her, perhaps even encouraging her. He hadn't realised, however, that she was seriously interested in him until he'd had a call from her on his mobile inviting him to meet her for lunch. Flattered and intrigued, after all Miriam was a stunning looking girl, so why not a bite of lunch. She was Vincent's second wife and he reckoned that maybe she was craving some male company more her own age for a change.

He'd gone to the office in the Bentley on the day Miriam had invited him to lunch driven by Brian his chauffeur. He'd given Brian the afternoon off and driven the car himself down the M3 to a small pub on the edge of the New Forest where he was to meet Miriam. It was after lunch that she had; well seduced him was the only way to put it. Making love with him in the back of the Bentley parked on a small gravel-pull in, the New Forest ponies the only onlookers. With the promise of more of the same Andy had become infatuated.

The meeting with Vincent Floyd the next day went better than Andy expected and in his view, fully justified the amount of money that had been spent on the evening at the Bridgedale. There had been agreement to a trial of the full range of Way of Life products in all of the fifty-five Floyd Chemist branches in the Greater London area. The sales would be monitored over a four-week period with a view to rolling out the range throughout Southern England.

Vincent had been full of praise for the products. "Shouldn't be telling you this, Andy," he tapped the side of his nose, "tried out the goat weed stuff myself; must say Miriam seemed satisfied and I know I was." He grinned and felt his face redden. "Life in the old dog yet."

Andy made a mental note to ask Miriam how it had been for her, am I getting jealous he thought to himself.

There was a final discussion about distribution and marketing and the meeting finished with Andy arranging to follow up with the Production Director. He needed to ensure that there would be a continuity of supply when the product sales took off, as he knew they would.

Chapter 3

Driving through the Berkshire countryside at 7.00am on a chilly morning in early October the dinner party of a few weeks ago was all but forgotten. Andy was on his way to see his horses exercise on the gallops and was driving at a steady seventy miles an hour on the motorway. The stables were located at the edge of the downs near Lambourn which was the traditional home of National Hunt racing. Set amidst rolling countryside, covered at this time of the year with a patchwork of rich, brown and newly ploughed fields, there were any number of racing stables. They ranged in size from extensive yards with stabling for a hundred or more horses to the smaller, local farmer, training his own horse on a permit from the Jockey Club. Adrian Fordham was a trainer who fitted neatly into the middle range. Moderately successful with racing stables not many miles from Lambourn in a small Berkshire village. His yard was called Yew House Stables. It was named after the ponderous but stately looking yew trees that guarded the entrance to the drive leading to the stables. Among the forty or so horses in his yard were six that he trained for Andy Clewer. In fact, Andy owned more horses in the yard than any other one person, most of the other horses being owned by partnerships or syndicates.

The first string was going out onto the gallops at 7.30am with Alternative Ways, Andy's 6-year-old gelding and the stable's rising star, doing one final piece of work before his race that weekend in a steeplechase at Uttoxeter racecourse. Summer jumping was over and the proper National Hunt season was underway.

Pulling up beside the office Andy was greeted by Jonny, the assistant trainer at Yew House. "Morning Mr Clewer, bit parky this morning;" Jonny stretched out his hand and opened the door of the Aston Martin Vantage that Andy had chosen to drive that day.

"The Guvnor's waiting for you in the Land Rover. The first string left the yard a few minutes ago." He pointed with his thumb toward the battered four wheeled drive vehicle parked beside the office.

Andy got out. "Morning Jonny, I think I'll put my boots on, don't want to tread horse crap all over the car's nice wool carpets." He opened the boot of the car and sat on the edge as he took off his loafers and dug out a pair of wellington boots and a wax coat that reached down to his knees. "I'm looking forward to a spot of breakfast after all the fresh air that I'll be forced to breathe out on those gallops. I hope Mary's got the AGA fired up."

"Don't worry Mr Clewer, she was well briefed that you were coming and she knows how to look after you." Mary was the seventy-five-year-old village lady who had worked in the yard as a girl when the stables had been owned by the local Lord of the Manor. It was where he used to keep his horses and a few hounds as part of the nearby hunt.

Andy walked across the yard nodding to one or two of the lads as they mucked out the loose boxes that had been vacated by the horses on their way to the gallops. Laid out like three sides of a square with an open end, there were thirty boxes in the main yard with another thirty contained in the big American barn that had been built alongside. One or two heads appeared over the top of the stable doors as the inquisitive occupants looked hopefully for a polo mint or a carrot.

"Hurry up Andy," called Adrian through the open window of the Land Rover, "the first lot's almost at the bottom of the all-weather and we need to get moving if you want to see AW do his stuff." Most of the horses in the yard were known by their nicknames rather than their full racing names. Alternative Ways was nicknamed AW, obviously based on the initial letters of his name. Another of Andy's horses had the nickname of GG, from his full name of Ginseng Ginger, although very apt for a horse. Andy's company sponsored all of his horses so as well as the jockey wearing the company logo on his silks the horses were all named to reflect products or product ranges. It made good marketing sense with so many races being televised, not to mention the fact that the VAT on the training fees and other expenditure could be claimed back.

"Sorry boys and girls, no time for you at the moment, the boss is calling me." Andy said to the horses as he walked briskly toward Adrian and the waiting Land Rover.

They turned out of the stable yard and drove down the lane for about 200 yards before veering onto a dirt track that led down the side of a forty-acre wheat field - now just a field of stubble waiting to be turned over by the plough. This was one of the many off road tracks and walkways that the riders used to take their equine charges from the stables to the gallops. It was safe and well away from any traffic that might otherwise frighten and spook the horses.

"This is his last piece of work before he runs at Uttoxeter on Friday," Adrian grinned, "I don't think there's anything in the race to worry him," he paused, "could you put a thousand pounds on for me?"

"Hmm, that confident are we," Andy thought for a moment, "Let's see him work the gallops and we'll talk on the way back for breakfast." The stable was a betting yard but it didn't do for a trainer to be putting fairly large sums of money onto horses he trained as it would give the game away that a horse could be expected to win and so reduce the betting odds. It was usual, in Adrian's case anyway, to ask the owner to place the bet. The owner put the money on – most owners had an account with one of the large bookmaking firms - and when the horse won, they passed over the winnings but kept the stake that they had put up. The yard picked up money without any outlay in the first place. If the horse didn't oblige, the arrangement was that any stake money owing would be deducted from the next winning bet. It worked well for both the owner and the trainer. The owner, confident that the trainer would not take any undue risks with his money, could place a large wager in the knowledge that it was as near as possible to a sure-fire thing.

They caught up with the string of ten horses just as they turned into the field where, at the bottom of the steep slope, the gallops started.

Adrian put his head out of the window as he slowed the vehicle down to keep up with the horses as they paced along on the track covered in wood chippings. He needed to give each of them their final riding instructions for the morning gallop. "Cowboy," he said to the small figure perched on the tiny saddle of a big rangy chestnut, "Mr Clewer wants to see your boy do a piece of fast work up along sides, give us five minutes to get up the hill and then you and

Aunt Sally come up at a canter. When you get back down, I want to see you come up at half speed. Pull up at the top and we'll have a look at you."

Terry, or Cowboy as he was known to everyone at the stables, was the travelling head lad, a good natured twenty-seven-year-old from nearby Newbury. "Guv," he responded gently kicking his heels against the horse's flanks to keep Alternative Ways moving forward. Like some of the employees in the yard, he rode out horses on the gallops when he wasn't taking one or more of them to the races.

After some more shouted instructions to the other work riders the Land Rover pulled away from the horses and ran over the turf beside the all-weather track that the horses would use for their exercise. The gallops were five furlongs long, that is just over a half mile, and rising gently at first, they steepened about two and a half furlongs from the end. It was a good workout and test for the horses and riders alike. Adrian brought the vehicle to a halt just past the halfway point and they both got out, their breath steaming in the fresh October air.

You could hear the horses before you saw them - so steep was the hill. The rhythmic beat of hooves, punctuated by the snorting breath of the horses, preceded the appearance of the thundering animals themselves.

Almost talking to himself Adrian named each horse and made comment about its action and the ability of the rider to follow the instructions they'd been given at the bottom of the gallops. "Here comes your boy now."

Andy took a small pair of binoculars from the pocket of his wax coat and raising them focused until the image of the horse and rider filled his eyes. "Looks like he's enjoying himself." Alternative Ways and the other gelding, Aunt Sally, flashed past the point where they were standing, the ground vibrating as a couple of tons of horseflesh went by in a canter. Reaching the top of the gallops both riders brought their mounts down to a walk and turning, began the trek downhill to do it all again but this time at half racing speed.

Andy's mobile phone rang and he moved back towards the Land Rover as he answered it. "No, I'm not tucked up in bed with something blonde to keep me warm," He laughed, "As a matter of fact I'm freezing my knick-knacks off in a field in Berkshire." He listened to the voice at the other end of the phone. "No don't worry everything will be in working order when I see you later. In fact, I'm looking forward to you warming me up."

He heard Adrian shout and realised that the horse would be on its way up the gallops for the fast piece of work and this he wanted to see. "Must go now see you at three, usual place, it's all booked, room two one three." He rang off without waiting to hear any response and hurried across to the edge of the gallops.

He found it difficult to keep the feeling of excitement out of his voice as he followed the progress of the two horses as they thundered up the hill. Although both were being kept in check by their riders his horse was eating up the ground with effortless strides that was leaving the other horse behind. So much so that, by the end of the gallops, Alternative Ways was a good fifty yards in front.

"Christ, Adrian, he's jumping out of his skin. I can see why you want to have a nice bet on him."

"Yeah, the ground's come just right and I think we should get fair odds about him. He didn't do anything wrong in his last race but he was well beaten and I think the bookies won't expect him to go too well. His blood count wasn't quite right that day but I had the vet test him yesterday and he's spot on. He is almost at the same weight as when he won at Newbury by six lengths, still on the bridle, remember?"

They got back into the Land Rover and drove back towards Yew House. Andy nodded, "Is this the big one Adrian?"

"No, he's entered at Cheltenham for the XYZ Handicap, if we back him to win that now, before Uttoxeter, we should get a good price. After Uttoxeter," Adrian grinned, "well let's say that everyone will know that we've got a hotpot on our hands after he's won doing cartwheels."

"He'd bloody well better win if we put some big money on or else he'll be pulling bloody cartwheels." Both men laughed.

The Land Rover bounced into the yard splashing through the mud and puddles caused from hosing down the horses after their exercise.

They were then dried off, rugged up and put back into their loose boxes. Adrian pulled up close to the office.

"Go in and get some breakfast, I'm going to check the horses and give instructions for the next lot." Adrian strode off across the yard to where the string of horses, steam rising from their flanks, was just coming up the track from the gallops.

"Sausages, bacon, fried bread, the works, Mary," shouted Andy as he marched through the office and into the kitchen that adjoined it. "In fact, I could eat a horse, as long as it's not AW."

Mary bustled across from the Aga where she had kept Andy's breakfast in the warming oven. "Don't you worry Mr Andy; those sausages are all pork straight from Lumley's the butcher. Is it toast and marmalade to finish?"

Andy nodded his mouth already full of succulent sausage. "Mary, you old tart, you know the way to a man's heart is through his stomach. Nobody cooks fried bread like you."

"Just you clear that plate and let me get on with the washing up. Here, toast, marmalade and I've made you a pot of coffee."

Mary placed a pot of coffee and a plate piled high with toast onto the table then went through into the utility room to start the washing up. Andy ate steadily. As he speared the final piece of sausage, dipped it into the last of the brown sauce, his thoughts turned to the conversation he'd had with Adrian about the horse's chances at Uttoxeter.

A decent winning bet would be useful right now. The bank had been on to him to reduce his considerable overdraft and had let it be known that, until he had, there would be no further funds available to him. He had his account with Leisure Industries and as he had settled his debts with them, he could put a bet on the horse for Cheltenham. Pulling his phone from his pocket he called up the client's free phone number for Leisure Industries.

"Account number AC7135," he told the voice that answered, "Password champagne."

The voice identified herself as Milly and asked how she could help.

"What price Alternative Ways to win the XYZ Handicap?" Andy tapped his fingers impatiently on the table as he waited to hear.

"Alternative Ways is showing at 3/1," said Milly, "he's currently third favourite at the moment.

"I'll take five thousand pounds to win at 3/1," Andy smiled, just like that and he should be picking up fifteen thousand pounds for this one simple phone call and of course he'd get back the money that he had staked.

In accordance with the policy of most telephone betting organisations Milly read the bet back and confirmed that it had been recorded to his account, thanked him and rang off.

Andy turned his mind to the horse's more immediate race. He had already used up his agreed credit limit backing the horse at Cheltenham. There was nothing else for it he would have to place a cash bet with a couple of the bookmakers on the rails at Uttoxeter if he was to make anything out of his horse's chance to win. Already confident of the horse winning, he was wondering how to spend the money.

He nodded to himself as though reaching a decision. "I'm off now Mary," he called toward the utility room where she was still washing and drying the breakfast things. "Thanks for breakfast, it was great."

With that he swept out of the door and made his way toward the box where AW now stood waiting for his breakfast as the lad tightened the girth on a rug that was covering the horses powerful back.

Cowboy straightened up and turned to greet him. "He looks and feels in top form Mr Clewer; I wish I was riding him on Friday. The Guvnor said he'll give me an advance on my wages so as I can get a few quid on him."

Taking his wallet from his pocket Andy took out a twenty pound note. "Here, have this one on me." He enjoyed playing the high rolling owner with plenty of money and the lads in the yard all thought of him as one of the best. He stroked the soft velvet muzzle of the big chestnut.

Reaching into his pocket he pulled out a packet of polo mints that he had picked up in the office. Adrian bought them by the box full so that owners could give their horse a treat when they came to visit. Holding a mint in the palm of his hand he pushed it toward the horse who, with a soft snort, daintily picked it off with his big rubbery lips.

He gently rubbed the horse's nose. "You just do the business on Friday AW and I'll buy you a whole stable load of mints." The horse tossed his head up and down several times before turning his attention to the packet of Polos still in Andy's hand.

Walking back to the car Andy opened the boot and threw in his wax jacket. Sitting on the edge of the car boot he eased off his by now muddy boots. These too he tossed carelessly into the boot and slipped on his loafers. Slamming the boot shut he opened the driver's door and got in.

As the car started with a throaty roar Adrian appeared from round the corner of the loose boxes a bridle in his hand.

"Had your breakfast I see - you'll be there on Friday?" he leaned on the door of the car as Andy let down the driver's window.

"Just try and stop me," he put his hand on Adrian's arm, "I'll bet with the bookies on the rail and see you right when we have a drink on the way back, that's if you're sure that he'll win."

"Don't worry, there's nothing in the field that'll get near us, just you make sure you get a good bet on at a good price for Cheltenham before Friday. Once he's won at Uttoxeter he'll be red hot for the XYZ."

With a wave Andy gunned the Aston Martin out of the yard and down the lanes toward the M4 wondering where he was going to get sufficient cash to put a bet on for himself and for Adrian.

He'd sort it he was certain, just as he was certain that he would enjoy himself later that afternoon. That is if the other afternoons together were anything to go by.

Chapter 4

The Aston Martin swept round the bends of the narrow lane that led down to the main road through to Hungerford. From there it was no more than a 5-minute run to junction fourteen of the M4.

Reaching the junction Andy turned eastwards and headed toward London. He had a lunch meeting in Reading with a marketing agent who sold his products in Scandinavia, an area he was keen to exploit. He saw the clean and healthy approach that the inhabitants seemed to take to life as an indication that they would receive his products well and early sales seemed to show that he was right.

Using his voice activated hands free car phone he made a call to the office. Debbie answered almost at once and he smiled knowing that his car phone number must have come up on the screen showing him to be the caller. "Morning Debbie, on the ball this morning, any messages?"

"Yes, morning Andy, two or three that can wait until you get in this afternoon and Don wanted an urgent meeting with you to go through the marketing account."

The smile slipped from Andy's face at the thought of the marketing account. "Put Don in the diary for next week, tell him that's the earliest I can do and Debbie I won't be in this afternoon." He paused as a lorry pulled out from the slow lane without any signals no more than 20 yards in front of him.

"You stupid twat," he yelled shaking his fist as he swerved the Aston Martin at 80 miles an hour into the outside lane. "Sorry Debbie, bloody lorry all over the motorway, I'm just on my way into Reading."

Debbie's voice filled the car through the loudspeakers, "Are you OK Andy"? She sounded concerned, "The messages aren't that important but can I get you on your mobile if I need you"?

"I'm fine. I'm working on a project and I don't want any interruptions, I'll call in later for an update and don't forget, put Don off until next week". With that he rang off not giving Debbie any time to question him further.

With time to spare before his lunch meeting, he decided to stop off for a cup of coffee at the Services just off the motorway at the Newbury junction. A slight drizzle was drifting across the car park as he pulled in. A space for disabled drivers stood empty right beside the doors to the service area and restaurants. Without hesitation Andy nosed the car into the space and switching off the engine reached over to get his jacket from the seat behind. He jumped out and hurried into the warmth.

Stopping only to buy a Racing Post from the news stand he made his way to the cafeteria where he bought a mug of coffee and sat at an empty table in the non-smoking area. He sipped at his drink and scanned the pages of the paper. An article by Inside Scout on next month's Cheltenham meeting caught his eye. 'XYZ Banker', said the headline 'Christmas has come early, get your bets on now'.

Inside Scout, the paper's main racing correspondent, had given his opinion of each of the 10 runners, rating their chances of carrying off first prize. Of Alternative Ways he had discounted any chance of winning, 'still an inexperienced horse who whilst improving has a lot to find to get anywhere near the favourite, well beaten last time out over this distance'.

Up yours thought Andy and he turned his mind to the little problem of getting hold of some money before this Friday's Uttoxeter race. He needed to borrow the money but obviously he couldn't share his information of the horse's well-being with just anyone as the word would get out. There was one person who he could trust and he was on his way to see her this afternoon.

A coach must have pulled into the services for suddenly the tables around him started to fill up. The noise level rose as children demanded crisps and cola from ragged looking adults who might have been parents or teachers. He finished his coffee and got up.

'Might as well pay a visit, never miss the chance my old mum used to say', he thought to himself and he made his way to the gents before getting back to the car and continuing the journey toward Reading.

His lunch meeting was to be in a pub called George and the Dragon, right in the heart of the town. Parking, always difficult in Reading was even harder when you had a car the size of the Aston

Martin. He pulled into the railway station forecourt, not an empty space in sight.

"Damn", he swore out aloud, with engine idling he sat there waiting. After about 6 minutes just as his patience was starting to wear thin a man hurried across the road from the direction of the town centre and headed toward a parked Jaguar S type.

Edging his car forward Andy was well placed to reverse into the vacant slot the moment the Jaguar pulled out. A cursory glance at the meter told him that parking was for 1 hour only with no return within 3 hours. Shrugging his indifference Andy put two one pound coins and a fifty pence piece into the machine and retrieved his ticket. Placing this on the top of the dashboard where it could be seen he slammed the door and activated the alarm. It was nearly ten minutes to one and the short walk would see him arrive about 10 minutes late. Just right to show them who's the boss.

Lunch was all about statistics, sales against targets and delivery costs, gross margins and commission rates. Overall, the Scandinavian business was holding up better than expected and Andy was well pleased. However, time was slipping away and at a quarter past two his mind was elsewhere. He was in fact thinking of a hotel bedroom about half an hour away.

Using the car park as his excuse Andy parted company with the agent and hurried back to the station. Although more than half an hour over his time there wasn't any parking ticket stuck to the windscreen or clamp on his front wheel. Pulling out of the car park he negotiated the one-way system and headed out of Reading toward A329 (M). He was heading for Egham and a hotel beside the river Thames near where the Magna Carta had been famously signed all those years ago.

When he arrived, there was a conference underway at the hotel so he had to park his car in the overflow car park. Still a conference meant that there would be plenty of people around and there would be less chance of anyone noticing him amongst a group of other businessmen.

He was quite right. When he walked into the hotel foyer it was a throng of sober suited men and women some heading out for the car park and a cigarette, others jostling this way and that so as to get the best signals on their mobiles. The conference had broken for afternoon tea.

Walking in a purposeful fashion Andy headed down the corridor and ignoring the lifts made his way toward the stairs. Two at a time he now hurried upwards. By the time he reached the second floor he was puffing and blowing. He stood, waiting for his heart rate to slow and his breathing to steady.

He gently tapped twice on the door of room 213, paused and then knocked harder another two times. He looked up and down the corridor and then as the door opened slipped quickly inside.

The curtains were drawn and the room was in semi darkness. The flowers and champagne he had ordered were on the small coffee table beside the bed with two tall crystal flutes already half full of the pale effervescent wine.

He took Miriam in his arms and held her tightly. She felt warm, her body soft and yielding, sheathed in a silken wrap, with the smell of heady perfume.

"M'mm, you feel good", he whispered, his breath ruffling the fine strands of hair that covered her ear.

She pushed him gently away from her. "Let me get that jacket and tie off you", her voice husky with emotion, "and then we can taste those bubbles you so thoughtfully arranged".

He slipped out of his jacket and she put her hands to his collar and undid his tie, slipping it from around his neck. Unfastening the top buttons, she slid her hands inside his shirt and gently rasped his chest with her fingernails.

He bent forward and took her head in both his hands kissed first the top of her head and down the side of her face until their lips met. She pressed her body against his and he felt her tongue pushing its way into his mouth.

He broke away from her. "I was going to say what about a glass of bubbly to get us in the mood but you seem to be in the mood already".

Miriam pouted, "I'm in the mood alright but a girl would never say no to a glass of champagne". She moved over and sat on the bed.

Picking up both glasses she held one out to him. "Come over here and enjoy a drink, it will give you energy", she gave a wicked smile.

He sat down beside her and took the offered glass. "Here's to a fun time and us". They touched glasses and drank.

Andy took the glass from Miriam's hand and put onto the coffee table. He stood up and stretched out his arms toward her. Taking her hands in his he pulled her to her feet. In the dim light he could just see the outline of her bra and panties beneath the soft sheen of the wrap.

He undid the tie that held the wrap together and slipped from it her. He bent to kiss her neck and shoulders at the same time letting his hands caress her back, moving down her body until he reached the swell of her buttocks. He pressed her towards him, letting her feel him against her. A low moan escaped from her lips and she eased away from him, her hands pulling impatiently at the buckle on his belt.

After making love they must have drifted off to sleep because it was nearly five o'clock and dark outside before he remembered that he had promised to ring Debbie at the office. He padded naked and barefoot across the room to pick up his trousers, where they had been thrown more than an hour and a half ago and retrieved his mobile.

"Office", he barked. The phone lit up and dialled Debbie's number. "Debs, it's me, everything OK"?

"I thought you'd forgotten, it's getting late in the day. Your wife rang and said don't forget that you've got a dinner party tonight and that you need to be home by five thirty".

"Buggeration, I completely forgot. Look, give her a call and tell her I'll be home by six. Anyone else want me?"

"Nothing that can't wait, that is if you're coming in tomorrow"? Debbie sounded fed up. Andy realised that it couldn't be much fun fielding calls and taking messages not knowing what her boss was up to or even where he was but still, that's what she got paid for.

"Don't worry I promise I'll be in and go through all the messages." Debbie interrupted him. "Andy, you chair the production meeting at 9.30, you have lunch with the graduate trainees and at 2.30 you're giving a talk to the Berkshire Primary Care Trust on the uses of alternative medicines. But don't worry I'm sure you'll fit me in".

Andy sat on the edge of the bed. "I know I've been hard to pin down but Debbie I'll be a good boy and make sure we spend some time going through everything".

Debbie laughed, "See you tomorrow, good boy, I'm just going to tidy up then I'm off home."

Andy lay back on the bed, which Miriam took as a sign to snuggle up to him. "You were a good boy, in fact you were a good big boy that stuff of yours really does work," she giggled "would you like me to be an advert for your horny whatsit."

"Don't be stupid. Look I forgot but we've got people coming to dinner tonight. Suzanne's already been on to the office, expecting me back home in half an hour, I'll have to go." Getting off the bed he moved toward the bathroom. "M'mm better have a shower first, wash off the smell of that perfume of yours. What is it called Seduction by someone or the other?"

Miriam sat up. "Yeah, it's new and as you can vouch for it works. Would you like me to come and scrub your back?"

"You'd better get dressed Miriam. No but I'll tell you what, I need to borrow two thousand pounds until next week, be an angel and lend me the cash." Andy moved through into the bathroom.

"I thought you were rolling in money." Miriam got off the bed and moved to lean on the bathroom door frame watching him as he pulled the shower curtain across the bath. "Anyway, what do you need it for?"

The shower was running and Andy stepped in. "I'm just short of ready cash until next week." He raised his voice over the sound of the shower; "The horse is running on Friday and I need to place a bet with the bookies on the course. Why don't you come with me; we can have some fun?"

"That sounds great," Miriam paused, "but what about Suzanne won't she be going with you?"

"No, she only likes to go to the big meetings where she can be seen on TV in the parade ring or picking up a prize in front of a big crowd - she'll never know. Make sure you get the cash and I'll pick you up from here, say half past eight Friday morning?" He switched off the shower and pulled back the curtain.

Miriam passed him a towel and stood frowning. "Yeah, that's good. Vincent is going to Leeds on Friday for a meeting with the regional managers, he'll be leaving early. He always goes by train, says it gives him time to read up on the figures. He won't be back until after nine o'clock, he's having dinner with some finance person or another."

Andy wandered into the bedroom rubbing his hair on the towel. Sitting on the edge of the bed he put on his socks, stood up and pulled on his pants and trousers before threading his belt through the loops. "I must love you and leave you, my darling".

He slipped on his shirt and tucking it into his trousers stuck his tie in his pocket; "Just drop the key at reception, they're sending the bill on to the company. I put it down as a meeting room. Well, we did meet didn't we?" He glanced in the mirror and ran his fingers through his hair. "That'll do." He nodded at his reflection and turned toward Miriam.

Kissing her tenderly on the lips Andy opened the door and stepped out into the corridor. Miriam waved his jacket at him. "I expect you'll need this?" She laughed, "See you a bit later on."

"What do you mean, see you later on?" Andy stopped and leaned back into the doorway.

"Vincent and I are coming to dinner, you'd forgotten, hadn't you? I bet you'll be surprised to see me?"

"Damn, of course it's you and Vincent and some plonker from our distribution company and his wife or mistress or something. Yes of course I'll be surprised. I shall probably tell you how radiant you look and how much I'd like to get into your knickers."

Miriam pushed him gently out the door, "I might not wear any tonight," she giggled and closed the door before Andy could respond.

"Don't forget the money on Friday," was Andy's last call through the closed door before he walked briskly down the corridor.

Chapter 5

The Clewers lived in the village of Crondall on the Surrey/Hampshire borders, not far from Farnham. The double fronted Edwardian house had been built as a vicarage and stood in two acres of garden - reached from the lane by a drive that stretched for almost a hundred yards. The drive ended in a sweep of gravel in front of the house with parking for six or more cars.

"I'm sure we turn left here," Miriam looked up from the piece of paper that had been faxed to Vincent's office with directions on how to find Greenacres, as the house was called.

Vincent slowed the car as they approached a cross roads. "Why anyone would want to live out here in the bloody sticks is beyond me," he indicated left and swung the Jaguar down the narrow lane, "if you'd got back on time from your ladies bloody keep fit meeting or whatever we wouldn't be in such a rush now. You know I like to be on time, keep the other fellow on his toes not arrive late all hot and bothered giving him the advantage."

"Vincent, we're out to supper not some business meeting, besides I'm looking forward to seeing Andy again."

"And Suzanne," Vincent snorted, "don't forget our hostess."

"How could I" Miriam retaliated, "with you fawning over her half the time, ogling her."

"Don't be so ridiculous," Vincent accelerated fiercely causing the car to leap forward at a dangerous pace, "I'm no more than friendly towards her, not like you with Andy, touching him all the time, whispering and giggling like a schoolgirl with the hots."

"Alright, alright, just slowdown will you I want to get there in one piece."

Vincent grinned. "Frightened are we, wetting our knickers then?" He eased his foot off the accelerator and the big car slowed to a more reasonable pace. He turned to look at Miriam. "What are you smirking at?"

"Oh nothing much, just you thinking I might wet my knickers, some chance of that. Take it easy now, I think that the entrance to their drive is somewhere around here. Yes here we are, white gate posts and a gravel drive, turn in here."

The car crunched onto the gravel and made its way down the long drive toward the house. Andy's Aston Martin and a big BMW stood parked to one side of the turning circle in the front of the house. As Vincent pulled in beside them the front door opened and Suzanne waited to greet them. He got out and walked round to the passenger door, opened it, helped his wife out of the car and kissed the back of her hand.

"All here in one piece." He smiled tenderly.

"Come in, come in," Suzanne called, "we are just having drinks, so you haven't missed anything".

"Sorry were a bit late," said Vincent giving Suzanne a peck on the cheek, "Miriam got in late from her keep fit class."

"Pilates actually," smiled Miriam as she blew a kiss toward their hostess and glanced round looking for Andy.

"This way, into the drawing room." Suzanne closed the front door behind them and they moved from the hallway, through double doors and into a room that was furnished with three sofas and numerous occasional tables. Each sofa was guarded by a softly lit standard lamp that bathed the room in a warm glow.

"Let me introduce you to Phil Manners and his partner Julie. This is Vincent and Miriam. Now what about a drink, gin and tonic?"

Andy came forward with two glasses in his hands. "Already anticipated." Smiling he handed over a glass to Miriam and bent to kiss her cheek. "My but you look good tonight, don't you think Vincent?"

"She always does, but then the amount of money she spends on clothes she blinking well ought to." Vincent took the glass of gin and tonic from Andy.

"A girl can't wear everything she buys, you know." Miriam winked at Andy and watched for his reaction.

He blushed at the thought of what Miriam might not be wearing. "Well it's good to see you both." He shook Vincent's hand. "Phil is MD of Support Logistics, our distribution company. Any complaints about deliveries to your stores and Phil's your man."

The three men gravitated together and for the next few minutes their talk revolved around business.

"Andy's right Miriam, you do look good, that Pilates must suit you, you're positively glowing." Suzanne gave a small laugh.

What with the champagne in the afternoon and now a very generous gin and tonic Miriam was feeling in an extremely light headed and frivolous mood.

"Well, I've been taking plenty of exercise you know. Why even this afternoon I was working flat out."

Before anyone could respond a jolly faced lady wearing a white apron stuck her head round the door. "Just ready to dish up Mrs Clewer. Perhaps you'd all like to go on through."

"Thank you, Polly. This way everyone." Suzanne led them out of the drawing room, across the hall and into a room where a gleaming oak table was set with six places. "This is the snug; I thought it cosier than the dining room. Now shall we sit boy girl, boy girl."

"Good idea." Andy pulled back a chair; "Julie you sit here, I'll be next to you, Miriam you'd better sit on my other side then Phil, then Suzanne and that leaves Vincent between Julie and you Suzanne. There, no one sitting next to their partner. Sit down everybody and I'll pour the wine." He moved to the sideboard where several bottles of red and white wine stood waiting. "White OK for everyone to start?" Before anyone had a chance to respond Andy began pouring white wine into the smaller of two crystal wine glasses beside each place setting.

Vincent patted the chair next to him. "Come on Suzanne come and keep me company. It'll do you good to get away from that husband of yours. I think you need an older man to look after you."

Suzanne nodded. "Why not Vincent, all I hear about is Horny Goat Weed it'll be good to talk about something else for a change."

"Damn good stuff actually." Vincent lowered his voice and bent close to Suzanne's ear. "Since Andy introduced it I thought Miriam and I should try it out. Must say it worked really well, I don't mean to be coarse but we went like the clappers, just the thing to perk up a flagging love life, you should try it."

"Ah I see. That explains why Miriam looks so good," Miriam smiled, "a satisfied woman."

Vincent glanced over toward his wife. "Well, we haven't, you know, done it lately but I suppose so."

Polly bustled in armed with a huge tray full of white bone china dishes and a soup tureen emanating steam and a heady smell bouillabaisse and garlic.

Miriam looked up at that moment and smiled across the table. Vincent held her gaze. 'She does look satisfied,' he thought, 'I wonder why.' He turned back to Suzanne. "Tell me what you get up to, Pilates, keep fit or some other girly pursuit?" He placed his hand on hers. "Anyway, I bet you look stunning in a leotard."

"No, she dabbles in art." Andy smirked at Suzanne. "Quite a budding Constable, aren't you my dear? Pass the bread Julie there's an angel."

"Oh, I say is that one of yours, its jolly good?" Julie Manners pointed to a watercolour picture of Tower Bridge with a Thames lighter heading against the tide.

"Well, it's one of my better efforts, at least it's one I can put on show." Suzanne blushed. "I really enjoy painting. I've got a small studio workshop in the garden. I potter about in there most days."

"I think you're being too modest my dear." Vincent raised his eyebrows. "Why I'd be more than happy to have a painting like that on the wall at home."

***

It was almost two hours later that they drifted back to the drawing room for coffee and after dinner drinks.

"Do you think I could go to the little girl's room?" Miriam glanced at Andy. "I really need to freshen up a bit."

"Of course, let me show you the way. There's a better mirror in the main guest en-suite than the downstairs loo, more light too." Andy stood up and guided her out of the room and making sure that he'd closed the door, led her upstairs.

They stood together just inside the main guest bedroom. "I've really got to check you know." Andy slid his hand down Miriam's waist and on down until he reached the hem of her dress. Slipping his hand under the dress he moved it upward. "You meant what you said then." Miriam moved against his hand and moaned softly.

"Andy," Suzanne called from downstairs, "we need some more brandy could you fetch another bottle?"

The mood was broken; Miriam pulled away and retreated into the bathroom turning to blow Andy a kiss.

"Of course dear, I was just on my way down." He ran lightly down the stairs and went through a door into the garage. Retrieving a bottle of Courvoisier Champagne Brandy from a cupboard just inside the door he walked back into the drawing room. "Now," pulling out the cork, "who wants a refill?"

It was after midnight when everyone had gone and Andy and Suzanne were getting ready for bed.

"You pay too much attention to that woman." Suzanne sat at her dressing table and smoothed moisturiser onto her face.

Andy wandered in from the bathroom. "Who?"

"You know who I mean, little miss flirty, Miriam."

"Just being polite to a good client's wife, there's nothing wrong with that. Anyway, you and Vincent seemed to be on very intimate terms. Secret whispers and holding hands, what was that all about?"

"That's all your fault. Vincent decided that they should try out the Horny Goat Weed. A great success according to Vincent, bonking like rabbits. I said no wonder Miriam looked good; she had the look of a satisfied woman. Vincent seemed to think that their night of passion was a while ago but still that stuff must be good."

Sliding into bed Andy turned out his bedside light. "When did they do it then? It must have been recently if she's looking, what did you say, satisfied."

"You're taking an interest all of a sudden. What are you going to do call it market research; no, I think she's seeing someone on the side, someone who's really able to satisfy her."

Andy lay in the semi-darkness, was he feeling jealous that Vincent was having sex with his own wife?

Suzanne got into bed. "Maybe we should try that stuff liven up our sex life. Let's face it you always say you're too tired, perhaps it will give you the uplift that you need." Laughing at her own joke she switched off her light.

"We could make a night of it, bottle of champagne, soft music, what do you think Andy?" She moved her hand down the bed to caress him.

"I've got to be in the office by eight, just let me go to sleep." He turned over letting her hand slide away from him.

She sighed. "I love you too."

***

Earlier that same evening Don Markham sat in his office. It was after six o'clock and most of the staff had gone. Only the cleaners were left and he made sure that they saw to his office first and then left him undisturbed at his work.

He was watching the computer monitor as he selected the log-in page from the menu. Punching in his password he accessed the finance master file and looked up the activity log for Andy's password. Only Don and the company IT Director had the authority to use the activity log.

"The bugger's been at it again." He said aloud. Don couldn't help himself the remark just slipped out. He looked up towards the door. No, it was OK, the door was closed and any way, who'd know what he was talking about. Even though he had the authority and the right to check the movement of finance through the company, when it came to checking on Andy, he always felt like it was spying – which of course it was.

Unlocking the middle drawer in his desk he took out a four-ring binder. The pages in the binder were separated by coloured dividers. He thumbed open the divider labelled 'Marketing'.

Behind the divider were several pages each containing a number of columns headed Date, Activity, Amount and Aggregate. Pausing only to check the screen once more Don made an entry onto the last page.

Settling your betting account old boy, he thought to himself. So far this year your extravagances have cost the marketing budget more than a hundred and twenty thousand pounds.

Locking away the binder, Don smiled to himself. Fifteen years ago, when the business was only just starting, Don thought Andy would make him a shareholder as well as an executive director. He had worked all hours setting up the financial controls and systems, driving hard bargains on leases and rents for the property and manufacturing plant. He thought he was carving himself a piece of the company only to be told by Andy - 'I don't think that's necessary, after all you get well paid and a good bonus'.

Don had been resentful but careful not to let it show. True he was well paid so why rock the boat. That hadn't stopped him from building up a dossier of Andy's shady manoeuvring of cash and outrageous expenditure over the years under the guise of business expenses.

Even though Andy acted as though he was the owner in reality it was the Company that owned and sponsored the horses, for that read paid for them, but not his betting or dubious entertaining. Don believed that the dossier was going to be the key to unlock the way to his getting a share in the company and needed the information to prove that Andy wasn't really fit to run the company. He may not have thought of it as blackmail but that was what it was, using the dossier as a lever to get what he wanted.

Chapter 6

"What are you up to today, my dear?" Vincent asked his wife as he straightened his tie in the dressing table mirror.

Miriam, still in bed, groaned from under the duvet. "God knows. What are you doing, it's still dark outside, and it must be the middle of the night?"

Vincent chuckled. "Never were an early bird were you. It's Friday, I'm off to Leeds to the regional meeting today, if you haven't forgotten." He looked at his watch. "The taxi should've been here by now. I'm catching the 8.07 from Kings Cross, should be back, oh, somewhere around 10 this evening." He turned toward the bed. "There's a cup of coffee for you on your beside table."

"I think I might do some shopping, maybe meet Suzanne Clewer for lunch and a gossip." Miriam sat up. "Pass me my wrap, there's an angel, is the heating on?"

"Yes it is on but it's only been on for about 20 minutes, bit of a frost out, first this month." Vincent gazed out of the window down onto the lawn. He wished that they could install double-glazing but their three-storey town house was a listed building and it was forbidden; so he continually moaned about the high cost of keeping the place warm and Miriam complained about the drafts.

"God, no wonder it's so cold." Miriam sipped at her coffee. "Are you ready to go then?"

Moving away from the window Vincent picked up his overcoat that was lying on the dressing table stool. "Yes my dear, I'm off as soon as the blasted taxi gets here," glancing once again at his watch, "the bugger's late, you know how I hate that."

"Yes I know. Now stop getting in a tizz darling and don't forget your briefcase it's on the hall table."

Walking across the room Vincent peered around the curtains at the road outside. "At last here he is. See you." Blowing a kiss toward Miriam he stalked out of the bedroom. She heard his hurried footsteps echo across the oak floored hall and the front door open and slam shut.

She sighed as the sound of the taxi pulling away from the house faded. Friday was race day. Now what did one wear to the races on a cold day?

Slipping out of bed Miriam shuffled into her slippers and wandered through to her dressing room. 'Trousers, definitely trousers and boots. The silk camisole, cashmere roll neck and my Persian lamb jacket, that should do it, oh and my matching Persian lamb hat.'

Feeling pleased at having made her choice so quickly, no dithering or changing her mind, she checked the time.

"Right," she said aloud, "just time for a shower, do my face and hair then into the car for Runnymede."

Soon she was ready to go but there was one more thing to do. She had visited the bank the day before and drawn out the money for Andy. It was hidden in a drawer in her dressing table so that Vincent shouldn't see it. She pulled out an envelope full of notes and stuffed it into her handbag before setting off.

***

Picking Miriam up from in front of the hotel on Friday morning Andy was in a buoyant mood even though Miriam was nearly thirty minutes late. His call to Yew House Stables from the car had elicited a positive thumbs up from Adrian Fordham. Alternative Ways was already en-route to Uttoxeter and as Adrian put it, bouncing out of his skin.

"My, my quite the little race goer, all you need is a pair of binoculars and you'd pass for the wife of an owner any day." Andy helped Miriam out of her coat, opened the passenger door and ushered her into the car. He placed her coat into the boot with his Crombie overcoat and felt trilby. It was just after 9.00am when he steered the Aston Martin onto the M25 and with effortless ease the powerful engine took them up to eighty miles an hour and into the outside lane. "Did you bring the money?"

"You don't waste much time in getting to the point do you. What if I hadn't, would you dump me on the hard shoulder?" Miriam clutched her shoulder bag protectively.

"Of course not," laughed Andy, "it's just that we can make a few bob today. The horse is bang on form and there's not much opposition in his race. I used up all the credit on my betting account to have a good wager on the horse at the Cheltenham meeting. I need to get today's bet on with the course bookies and that's got to be in cash."

Opening up her bag Miriam pulled out the envelope and waved a handful of fifty pound notes toward Andy. "I hope I get a drink out of this as well as my money back."

"My darling when the horse wins you shall have champagne. You can bathe in it if you want."

"M'mm, I just love the smell of leather." Miriam settled back in her seat and sniffed the heady air of the grained leather. "Will I be allowed into the parade ring and winner's enclosure and you know, pat the horse and jockey?"

"With an owner's badge on that nice fur coat of yours you can go anywhere, and for that two thousand quid, today, you are an owner."

Eating up the miles the journey to the racecourse set in the Staffordshire countryside passed quickly in the sumptuous comfort of the Aston Martin. Stopping only for a quick cup of coffee and a natural break, Andy's estimate of a two and a half hour journey was only out by ten minutes and they arrived in the owners and trainers car park around about a quarter to eleven.

"Perfect timing; I'm ready for a stroll around, I've booked us a table for lunch in the Platinum Suite Restaurant." Andy stretched his arms out and wriggled his back. "I could also use a beer."

They got out of the car and opening the boot donned their coats. "Must put on the trilby and look the part. We need to pick up our badges over there." Andy pointed to a doorway that stood to one side of the main entrance. Slinging his binoculars over his shoulder they walked briskly in the chill October air and entered the door. Andy showed his owner's pass card and asked for two badges.

The card was swiped through the computer. "Mr Clewer, Alternative Ways in the third race." The girl behind the desk sorted two badges and two race cards. "Good luck sir," her attention already turning to the next owners through the door.

Andy looped a badge through the buttonhole of Miriam's fur coat. "This way." He took Miriam's arm and led her round past the Staffordshire Stand with its private boxes and headed for the Owners and Trainers Bar located right beside the paddock and winner's enclosure. The day was bright but there was a chill wind blowing and they were glad to get into the warm fug of the bar.

"My God," Andy waved his hand in front of his face "look at all this lot vaping, it's enough to put you off your drink. Go and find a seat and I'll get us a drink; how about a glass of bubbly?"

"Don't you want to wait until the horse wins, then you can really let your hair down?"

"Well, perhaps you're right and I've got to get you back in one piece before the old man gets home. You have bubbly and I'll just have a sparkling water and pretend."

Walking over to the bar Andy caught the eye of the barmaid who had just finished serving another customer. "A glass of champagne and a fizzy water."

"Complimentary coffee or tea and a sandwich for owners." She sniffed. "Or you can have a pastry instead of a sandwich."

"Just the champagne and the water if you don't mind." He turned to see that Miriam had found a table that although cluttered with empty glasses was unoccupied.

Paying for the drinks Andy took them over and sat down. "Why don't you let me have that cash whilst there's not too many people around? I shan't put the bet on until the bookies get the prices on the board, you know just before the race."

Miriam sipped at her champagne and putting down her glass opened her bag and took out the envelope. "If this horse doesn't win my life will be hell. This is the money Vincent gave me to buy myself a pair of earrings for my Christmas present. Are you sure it's a dead cert?"

Andy looked quickly round and grabbed her arm. "Keep your voice down you silly idiot. With all these people around if any one sees the stash notes and hears you talking about dead certs it'll look very suspicious." He hissed, the words coming out between clenched teeth. "Yes of course I'm sure it'll win now let me just put the money away and we'll go and get our lunch; drink up and get ready to smile in the winner's enclosure."

Miriam didn't like being called a silly idiot but Andy took no notice as she glared at him.

They made their way down past the seafood bar and the weighing room to the Platinum Suite Restaurant. Situated on the first floor of the grandstand it offered the race goer a five course lunch and the table for the afternoon. With access to a viewing terrace and a big screen, the restaurant was the ideal place for those who wanted to be close to the action but with a degree of creature comfort. They were greeted at the door and shown to a table near the back.

"No, no," Andy shook his head, "this won't do - we need a table at the front where we can see what's going on. Look there's one over there set for two."

The restaurant manager consulted the list that he was holding. "I'm sorry sir but someone has particularly asked for that table, it wouldn't be possible to move you. The restaurant is full today."

Andy opened his wallet and took out a twenty pound note. "Are you sure we can't have that table?"

The manager looked at the note and back down at his list. "I seem to have got your booking mixed up sir. Your table is this one down at the front, just follow me."

Leading the way the manager seated them at their table. Beckoning him to lean down Andy held up the twenty pound note. "Do yourself a favour and put it on my horse, Alternative Ways, in the 3 o'clock."

The note disappeared from his hand as if by magic. "Thank you sir, I'll make sure that you're well looked after."

True to his word the service they received throughout lunch was excellent. At one point the manager came over; "Is everything alright Mr Clewer?"

Nodding Andy sent the man on his way. "Must have looked up the race card to find out who I was," he smiled. "Probably I'm the biggest owner here." Looking round he pulled a face. "Look like farmers most of them probably bred the horses themselves." He put his hand on Miriam's and gave it a gentle squeeze. "Now you see why I'm so confident that we'll win, after all, Alternative Ways wasn't bred in some farmyard. Cost me sixty thousand guineas to buy." He still thought of the horses as his own although he knew full well that the Company had paid for them.

Miriam just sat and smiled.

Chapter 7

The first race had already been run whilst they were finishing their meal and Miriam had managed to back the winner on the Tote. "You see," she boasted, "you're not the only one to make money on the horses. Take me down to the bookies and I'll reinvest on the next race."

"Come on then. Pick up your race card and let's go and sort out your next sure fire winner. We'll watch the race in the owners and trainers bar and catch up with Adrian before he goes to saddle AW."

Leaving the table they made their way downstairs. With Andy leading they struggled through the jostling crowd of people that thronged the area in front of the bookmaker's stands. It was as if everyone was watching and waiting, their eyes darting from one bookmaker's board to another until they found the price they wanted for their horse. Then it was a swift surge forward before the price could change. Thrusting their money at the bookie they would name the horse and the amount they were betting.

Miriam glanced at her race card. "Ooh look Andy, I've just got to back this one, it's called Misatisfied, it could have been named after me the other afternoon, or would that have been Mrs Satisfied. Anyway," she giggled, "let me bet my ten pounds."

"Bloody outsider," Andy grunted; "look at its form a row of zeros. It's never even been placed recently. Typical bloody woman backing a horse because you like its name, thought you'd have more sense. I suppose I might have known you'd be like all the rest."

"Never mind, that bookie has it showing at odds of twenty five to one. I think I'll back it with him." His barbed remark had hurt but still she moved forward and pushed the note out. "I'd like to put my ten pounds on number seven please, Misatisfied." She smiled at him.

Taking her money the bookie intoned, "Misatisfied two hundred and fifty pounds to ten, ticket number five four seven."

The clerk keyed in the information into a computer and pressed a button to issue the ticket.

"Keep that ticket safe my love, no ticket no pay out." The bookie passed her the numbered ticket with the name of his firm on it printed in bright red and green and turned to the next eager punter pushing money toward him.

Taking Miriam's arm Andy led the way round the parade ring to the owners and trainers bar.

There was a racecourse official standing outside the door checking the badges and barring entry to any who were not sporting the correct one. He opened the door as they approached. "Good afternoon, sir and madam."

Nodding his thanks Andy strode into the bar and looked round for Adrian, his trainer.

"Andy, over here." Called a voice raised above the chatter and noise of the crowded room. Adrian waved his cap above the heads of the group gathered in front of the big screen. He had secured a couple of bar stools and had two glasses on the shelf that ran along the side wall.

"I didn't realise you'd be bringing anyone, I'll go and get another drink." He turned toward the bar.

"It doesn't matter Adrian, I'll go without, I'm driving but I'll have some champagne after our boy has done the business. By the way, this is Miriam, a friend of mine."

Adrian took off his cap and leaned forward to give Miriam a peck on the cheek. "Andy's leading you astray is he?"

Miriam blushed wondering whether Andy had told him of their relationship. "I'm don't know what you mean." She almost stammered not quite sure what to say.

"You've been backing horses." He nodded at the numbered ticket that she still held in her hand.

"Oh that," she shrugged. "I managed to win ten pounds on the Tote in the first race and have backed an outsider to win in this one."

Adrian passed her a glass. "Better not to waste it, whisky and water is that OK? Look at one of the screens, the horses are just coming under orders." He pulled out a bar stool. "Here, sit down next to me and watch the race."

Miriam took a quick gulp of the drink as the voice of the racecourse commentator announced that they were under starters orders and 'they're off'. The noise in the bar quietened as the tape flew back from the starter's rostrum and the jockeys launched the horses toward the first of the eight hurdles. She watched and listened intently to the commentary. Misatisfied only managed to jump two hurdles before falling. Miriam lost all interest in watching the remainder of the field gallop on and concentrated on her drink instead.

"Bad luck," Adrian shook his head, "the word round the ring is that the favourite should romp home." About 3 minutes later Adrian was proved right as the favourite cleared the last hurdle two lengths in front of the nearest challenger and held on to win comfortably.

"We're in the next so I'm going to have to leave you and go and check on AW." Adrian eased off the bar stool; "See you in the parade ring. Have you," he hesitated, "you know made an investment." He glanced at Miriam.

"Oh don't worry Miriam knows all about it," Andy patted her arm; "I'll get down to the betting ring and see if I can get a good price."

They walked out of the bar together before splitting up to go in different directions, Adrian heading for the pre-parade ring and Miriam and Andy to where the bookmakers had their stands.

The bookmakers were just starting to put up the prices for the race and Alternative Ways was showing at odds of four to one.

Andy scanned the rows looking at the bookmakers boards with the betting odds. "Bit early yet there's no one betting. You wait and they'll push the prices out a bit to get the punters interested. There's 25 minutes before the off so we've got about another 15 minutes before we need to get into the parade ring and meet the jockey."

He nodded toward them. "Many of the bookies limit the size of the bets they take. The smaller one man firms won't accept a bet of two thousand pounds on a horse at four to one." As they watched the price for Alternative Ways on many of the boards changed to five to one.

Andy turned toward the rails that divided the different enclosures. That was where the big, national firms of bookmakers had their representatives. They made their way over.

The prices were changing almost constantly now. Wagers were being made with bookmakers altering their prices according to the market. Walter Coles was the name of one of the biggest firms of bookmakers in the country. As they studied the prices on his board the price for Alternative Ways was still showing at five to one.

Andy moved forward. "Alternative Ways two thousand pounds to win." He held out the bundle of notes.

Without a second glance the bet was repeated and the ticket issued and passed to Andy. The price however, after Andy's bet changed to three to one making the horse second favourite.

"Come on; let's get over to the parade ring." Andy took Miriam's arm and guided her through the crowds to the parade ring guarded by yet another official who checked their badges before letting them through.

Nearly all of the ten runners were already in the ring, stalking majestically round, occasionally eyeing the faces of the rows of people that surrounded the rails, or tossing their heads and snorting. One or two were really on their toes, almost skipping as they were led round and the lads and girls who walked them round, guiding them on a short rein, struggled to keep them in line.

Andy and Miriam walked onto the green turf in the middle of the ring and watched as Alternative Ways entered. He looked marvellous. His coat shone and Patty, the girl who looked after him, had brushed his hindquarters with a pattern of diamonds. He totally ignored the noise and bustle round the ring and strode calmly besides her occasionally turning his big head to look at something, or someone, who had caught his eye as round and round they went.

Adrian hurried across the grass and reaching Andy and Miriam raised his hat. "Got to play the part of the faithful trainer," he quipped, "the jockeys will be out in a couple of minutes. Is this a first for you Miriam, I mean being an owner at the races?"

"Oh yes and I'm really loving it. Look at all those people watching and wishing they could be in here with us."

"He's looking really well, Adrian," Andy nodded to the big display board that showed the latest betting odds for the race, "and it's not only me that thinks so he's five to two joint favourite now."

There was a sudden flurry of activity as the jockeys entered the ring in a kaleidoscope of colour and sought out the trainer and owners for whom they were riding. Wayne Packard was Adrian's stable jockey and he strode confidently toward them wearing Andy's racing silks of navy blue and emerald green diamonds with an emerald green cap.

He raised his whip and touched his forehead before shaking hands with Andy and Miriam. "Good afternoon sir, madam." Miriam was surprised that he was quite tall, she had always thought of jockeys as being tiny, about four feet six inches tall and she remarked on this to Wayne.

"That's the boys who ride on the flat," he grinned "they need to be able to ride at very light weights whereas we ride at around ten stone and upwards. In fact we're carrying ten stone twelve pounds this afternoon."

"Right Wayne," Adrian got down to business, "let them jump off and keep him about midfield for the first circuit. Bring him wide for the last three fences; the ground's a bit better over there. Once he sees daylight he'll want to go and you should be able to pick off anyone in front of you between the last two. I'm expecting you to come home clear. You shouldn't have to be hard on him, just do enough to win." A bell rang. This was the signal for the jockeys to mount.

"Right boss," Wayne pulled on his riding gloves and looked round for his mount. All of the horses had been turned from the path that ran round the outer edge of the parade ring onto the grass in the centre. Jockeys and trainers moved hurriedly to find their horses and once the jockey had been legged up into the saddle the horses were once again led round.

With a few minutes before the off time a gate was opened at the entrance to the racecourse proper and the horses began to file out.

Andy took Miriam's arm. "Come on we'll go over to the owners' viewing stand right in front of the winning post, Adrian will join us once he's seen the horse off onto the track."

They pushed and thrust their way through the multitudes of people. Some were heading for the Tote windows to get their bets on and some were hurrying to the lifts and stairs that would take them to the hospitality boxes and suites. Others just wanted to get a good position in the grandstand so as to watch the race.

"It's just two minutes away from off time and the starter is up on his box." The voice of the announcer boomed out of the loudspeaker positioned above where they were standing.

The race was a two mile steeplechase and the start was in the middle of the course turning left-handed to pass the grandstands with a complete circuit in front of the runners. From the owners' stand Andy raised his binoculars and watched as the horses began to arrive at the start. A breathless Adrian climbed up the steps to join them. The jockeys, keeping the horses off the course until called forward, walked them round in circles to ensure they stayed warm.

The starter called them out onto the course. At the jockeys' urging the horses moved forward through the gap in the white painted rails. For a few seconds horses were facing this way and that. The starter raised his arm and they sorted themselves out into a line across the course, jigging and stepping as they were held in check by the jockeys who called out to the starter when their excited horses turned and faced the wrong way. Exactly on race time the starter gave a shout. "Jockeys," at the same time he released the tape that had been stretched across the track and the horses eagerly broke into a gallop as it flew back.

Jumping the first fence Alternative Ways was up with the leaders but by the time they reached the second Wayne had dropped him back into eighth place. He was still there as they passed the stands and headed back out into the country.

The commentator had only mentioned him once as 'the other joint favourite is well down the field' paying more attention to the leading three horses that continued to force the pace and were slowly drawing clear.

As they went down the back straight Wayne started to make his move. It was not missed by the commentator who informed the crowd, 'Alternative Ways is moving through the field and taking closer order', much to Miriam's delight.

It was at the last fence that Wayne asked the horse for an all-out effort. He cruised up beside the leader both horses taking off together.

Alternative Ways landed half a length to the good and full of running. By the time they reached the winning post he was five lengths clear and Wayne was easing him down.

Adrian dashed off to meet the horses as they came off the course and down the walkway to the parade ring.

Miriam hugged Andy and they jumped up and down together. "We did it, we did it," Miriam squealed excitedly, "come on I want to be in the limelight and help you get your prize."

Laughing they pushed their way toward the winner's enclosure past happy punters with winning tickets and the not so happy who had backed some other horse.

The rest of the afternoon seemed to pass in a blur to Miriam. They stood in the winner's enclosure with the horse, jockey and trainer and had numerous photos taken. A man with a microphone came up and interviewed Andy and Adrian, questioning them about the horses chances at Cheltenham the following month. Several reporters, armed with note books, listened intently to the confident comments that both men made regarding the Cheltenham race. Andy went up to receive the trophy of a crystal whisky decanter and the congratulations of the sponsors. Calling Miriam to join him they smiled for the cameras whilst Adrian, having received a magnum of champagne as the winning trainer, went off to look after the horse. The next race was just starting as they made their way back to the owners' bar.

"I could get used to this," Miriam offered her empty glass for a refill. "Don't forget we've got to go and see that bookmaker, what's his name?"

"How could I forget that", Andy took another mouthful of champagne, "we'll finish this bottle and then go and collect."

***

They were on their way home. Andy having convinced the bookmaker to pay him out in cash they had been able to meet Adrian at the motorway services and pass him his winnings. Miriam had her two thousand pounds back and Andy had the rest, five thousand pounds, burning a hole in his pocket.

They were on the motorway and heading down toward London. "Why don't we have a bite of supper before I drop you off at Egham?" Andy glanced at Miriam. "What time are you expecting the old man back from his trip?"

"Oh, I don't know, about 9.30 or perhaps a little later, he's meeting someone for dinner, some finance guy."

"Well there you are then," Andy smiled, "supper it is."

Miriam reached forward and switched on the CD player. The soft voice of Norah Jones filled the car and they drove in companionable silence, Andy concentrating on keeping the powerful car moving at a steady eighty five miles per hour and Miriam lying back, eyes closed letting the music wash over her.

They reached Egham at 6.45pm. Andy parked the car at the back of a small seafood restaurant just off the high street and they walked hand in hand round to the front entrance.

"Do you have a table for two," Andy looked round at the early evening diners who occupied about a third of the restaurant.

The manager picked up two menus and guided them to a corner table. Pulling out two chairs he helped them get seated. "Can I get you something to drink?"

Andy glanced at the wine list. "Just bring a bottle of the Chablis, that'll be fine." With money in his pocket he didn't bother looking at the prices.

Miriam moved her chair round so that she and Andy were sitting almost side by side. "M'mm, this is cosy," she whispered. Letting her hand rest on Andy's leg she began to gently squeeze and rub the inside of his thigh.

"Would you like to try the wine, Sir?" The waiter placed an ice bucket beside the table.

"No I'm sure it'll be fine, just pour if you would."

Waiting until the wine had been poured; Andy handed one glass to Miriam and picking up his own glass, lifted it toward her. "Here's to a profitable day's racing, may there be many more."

He felt Miriam's hand on the zip of his trousers. She smiled at him and raised her glass with her other hand. "Here's to an added bonus."

"Are you ready to order yet Sir or should I come back later?" A young girl stood with her order pad smiling at Andy.

"Oh yes," Miriam leaned toward Andy, her hand deftly working his zip, "I know exactly what I want, how about you Andy?"

Andy struggled to control his voice, "Yes I think we'll both have crab bisque to start followed by the lobster thermidor. Can you serve that with a green salad?"

"No problem sir, as we cook to order it'll take about twenty minutes I hope that's OK?"

Miriam smiled at the girl, "That's fine we need a bit of time to ourselves anyway."

The girl moved away toward the open plan kitchen where the diners could see the chefs at work.

"Miriam, you really must behave yourself." Andy managed to remove her hand from inside his trousers without giving the game away. He surreptitiously did up his zip.

"I just thought you might like to know what you'll be missing tonight, you know a real celebration of today's win."

"If you want to do that I'm sure we can find somewhere." Andy squeezed her hand.

Taking a sip of her drink Miriam looked round the restaurant. "It's nice here, not too crowded and at least the tables are not close together, I hate that."

The crab bisque arrived, a rich caramel colour with a swirl of cream. The aroma was divine, a heady scent of the crab and brandy.

"Do you know I'm really quite hungry?" Andy attacked the steaming liquid. "This is excellent." His voice muffled by the slice of granary bread and butter that he had just stuffed into his mouth.

They had finished the meal by eight o'clock. "I'd better take you back to your car so that you can get home in plenty of time." Andy glanced at his watch. "Look, with that nice windfall today why don't we see about a trip somewhere; pamper ourselves somewhere warm?"

"Sounds good but what about Vincent and Suzanne?" Miriam pulled a face. "It'll be hard to get away without them knowing."

"Oh, we'll think of something, what about Dubai? The Royal Palace Hotel is right on the Juremiah beach with sun loungers laid out along the edge of the water, you'd love it."

"If we can get away with it." Miriam closed her eyes. "I can almost feel the sun on my back now."

"Right I'll fix it. Isn't Vincent going to that retail conference in Switzerland for a few days, why don't we do it then?"

Miriam stood up. "OK, but I'd better get going, I'll nip to the loo and then you can take me back to my car."

Andy waved to the waitress as she passed. "The bill please." By the time Miriam returned Andy had paid and was waiting for her by the door.

Driving the short distance from the restaurant to the hotel car park only took a few minutes. Slipping his arm round her, Andy gently kissed Miriam's lips. "It's a pity there isn't time for you to finish what you started in the restaurant." He pressed her hand down on his leg.

"I need to get back before Vincent. Think what we can get up to in Dubai." Miriam opened the door of the Aston Martin. "Give you a call on your private number early next week." She blew him a kiss and slamming the door shut, walked over to her own car.

Andy sat and watched her drive away. Thinking of her hand inside his trousers, he felt himself getting aroused once again - maybe Suzanne would be in luck tonight.

Chapter 8

Vincent Floyd sat in the lounge of the Park Plaza Hotel in Leeds less than five minutes' walk from the railway station. The meeting with the regional managers had gone well and he had left the Operations Director to wind up the session on the autumn sales campaign. Products from Clewer Alternatives had featured strongly on the agenda and had been received enthusiastically by the assembled managers.

With a tray of coffee and biscuits Vincent had plenty of time to catch his train and relaxed with the Daily Telegraph crossword. The television in the corner of the lounge was a slight distraction and he glanced up occasionally at an early evening news bulletin.

Twelve down was proving difficult, an anagram that he was working on and he barely registered the newscaster mention the name Andy Clewer.

It was a sports report and by the time he looked up he caught a fleeting glance of Andy at the races receiving a presentation, a woman standing beside him looking down at the trophy, before the face of the presenter filled the screen. He put down the paper and listened as the presenter went on to explain how Andy's horse had been made favourite for the XYZ Handicap at Cheltenham.

Vincent had glimpsed the woman standing there and for one moment she reminded him of his wife but of course it couldn't have been, she was out with Andy's wife. It must have been one of those attractive girls the sponsors of races use to adorn the presentations. 'What did they call them? Ah yes, I know, "eye candy".' He checked his watch. It was time to make a move and stroll down to the station.

Twenty minutes later he sat back in his reserved first class seat as the inter-city express pulled out of Leeds at exactly a quarter past five for the journey back to Kings Cross. He contemplated his meeting that evening with Don Markham. The meeting had been arranged without Andy's knowledge, Don had been insistent about that. Vincent had a gut feeling that the meeting might prove to his advantage. Following his gut feelings had served him very well over the years. He rested his head against the cushioned seat. His eyelids slowly drooped and he drifted to sleep as the rhythm of the wheels on the track lulled his senses.

It was just after seven thirty as he stepped into the cab outside Kings Cross. Don had booked a table in the Cellar Bar at a private club where he was a member. At that time of night it didn't take long before he was entering the club on Pall Mall.

Don had arrived early and sitting at his reserved table had ordered drinks for them both. Slightly rotund with a receding hairline he looked every inch the accountant that he was. With an ability to read and manipulate figures he had ensured that Clewer Alternatives continued to show consistent profit growth year on year. And yet Andy still wouldn't let him have a share in the equity of the business. Normally a quiet and affable man he felt a growing resentment toward Andy that had culminated in his arranging this meeting. The outcome meant a lot to Don although he was nervous as to how Vincent would react to the proposals he would put to him. He'd rehearsed in his mind the approach he would take and as he looked round the bar his confidence had been bolstered by a second gin and tonic when Vincent was shown to the table by the restaurant manager.

"I took the liberty of ordering a gin and tonic for you." Don rose as they shook hands and nodded toward the glass set opposite. "I expect it's been a long day, they usually are."

Vincent settled into his seat and raised his glass. "A welcome sight Don and how are you? Still, crunching the numbers for Clewer?" He picked up the menu and gave it a cursory glance.

"Always with an eye for the bottom line - which is really what I want to talk to you about." Don leaned forward and lowered his voice. "Look we go back a long way. Maybe I should have joined Floyd's Chemists instead of Clewer Alternatives when I had the chance. Who knows perhaps you would have cut me in and let me have a piece of the company? That's what I thought Andy would do but it hasn't worked out like that."

Vincent held up his hand. "I hope you haven't dragged me here to moan about the fact you're not a shareholder. It's Andy you need to talk to not me."

A waiter appeared at their table. "Are you ready to order gentlemen? "I'll have the bavette steak and chips." Vincent handed the menu to the waiter.

"I'll have the same and a bottle of the house claret." Don looked at Vincent. "That alright with you?"

"Yes this G&T is about finished and I'll be getting a taxi home." Vincent frowned. "Now what's all this about."

"Just to advise you gentlemen, the bavette steak is on the rare side so I hope that will be fine?" Both men nodded their assent.

Don looked directly at Vincent. "I need your assurance that is will be strictly between us?"

"This sounds cloak and dagger, but yes just between us." Vincent nodded.

The sommelier glided smoothly up to their table and held out a bottle of claret for Don to view.

Don nodded as he glanced at the label. "Yes thanks that's fine, just pour would you please?"

The claret was offered and poured with great panache and the sommelier withdrew leaving the two men sipping their wine, for a few moments not speaking but concentrating on flavour and depth of the wine.

Vincent broke the silence. "Well, out with it. What's so secret that we need to meet without Andy knowing?"

Before Don could reply the waiter appeared and set down two plates in front of them. "Bavette steak, béarnaise sauce and chips with a watercress salad. Can I get you anything further?"

"No thanks we're fine." Don took a sip of his wine before replying and paused until the waiter had moved away. "He's taken about 120k out of the business this year for his own ends, gambling and womanising." He shrugged his shoulders. "I know that he's in debt up to his eyes and I think I can see a way for me to get a share of the business;" He paused; "but I need help, in fact your help."

Vincent laid down his knife and fork. "Why should I help you? I've just done a good deal with Clewer Alternatives and look to make some fair profit; I'm not going to rock the boat, besides which we've become quite friendly."

"I think we'll both benefit if you just hear me out." Don pulled a piece of paper from his inside jacket pocket. "He had to put up his shareholding in the company as collateral for a £750,000 loan when he bought the house at Crondall last year then mortgaged the house to get his shares back." Don watched Vincent's reactions carefully. "He's been spending money like water and I know the bank have been chasing him to reduce his overdraft. I'm certain with the information I've got," he pulled a sheet of paper from his inside pocket and tapped the paper with his finger, "about the way he's abused company assets he'll agree to doing a deal with you on buying some of his shareholding at a good price. He needs to get out from under all this debt, I know he does."

Vincent looked at the food on his plate and dropped his knife and fork with a clatter. "I'm sorry Don, I'm not prepared to play ball. Andy's a friend and as I say we've done a deal that suits me. I'm not about to shaft him and that's it." He pushed his plate away, the meal half eaten. "I think I'd better go."

He stood up. "As you say this conversation goes no further. But I won't pretend that I'm happy about the way you're thinking, Don. You've done OK over the years. Just remember it was Andy that had the ideas that got the company up and running and that have made it a success. I know you've worked hard but its Andy that's taken all the risks." Turning he walked across the room and out of the door.

Don sat frowning at his drink wondering if he'd done the right thing in bringing his proposition to Vincent Floyd. He needed Vincent on his side. Perhaps he should have waited a bit longer.

***

Miriam had just closed the front door when she heard the sound of a vehicle pulling up outside the house. She still had her coat on when Vincent put his key in the lock and walked into the hall.

"Hello darling, you're back early." Miriam tried to sound casual but she hadn't expected him back until later. By then she would have changed out of the clothes she had worn to the races and have been settled in front of the television.

"Oh yes, dinner didn't go on as long as I thought." Vincent was still preoccupied by his conversation with Don otherwise he might have realised that his wife had just come in. "How's your day? Spent plenty of money?"

"No we just mooched about the shops, Harrods, Harvey Nicks, you know just the usual. We had lunch at Fortnum and Mason's." Miriam called over her shoulder as she started to climb the stairs. "Pour me a glass of wine there's a dear."

Vincent wandered into the kitchen and opened the fridge. "Australian chardonnay do you?" He shouted through the kitchen door. "What have you had for supper?"

He could hear Miriam moving around upstairs as he poured a drink for them both.

"I had rather a large lunch; I thought I'd just have a bite of cheese." She came down the stairs and into the kitchen. "Shall I put the telly on?"

Vincent laughed. "Thought I saw you on the box today. Some race or other that Andy Clewer's horse won. When they gave the trophy on that stand thing after the race there was a girl who could have been you. Mind you I only caught a fleeting glance. His horse is red hot favourite to win a big race next month."

Miriam choked on her drink. "Gosh, that went down the wrong way," she spluttered.

Switching on the set Vincent changed channels. "It was on the news, the sports section. The news is on in 10 minutes maybe we'll see it again."

His back was toward her so he didn't see the look of panic on her face. "Oh darling must we. I wanted to see the last part of the thriller on channel five. I can't possibly miss it."

Shrugging Vincent turned to face her. "I suppose so. I'm going up to get changed and then I'll be in the study for a while. Probably have a bath and go to bed. Don't stay up too long."

He kissed her on the cheek and she breathed a sigh of relief as he left the room. Going to the races had been fun but she couldn't afford to get caught out like that.

Chapter 9

Miriam picked up the phone and dialled the number for her husband's office. Vincent's secretary answered.

"Hello Janet, Miriam Floyd here. Is Vincent around?" She tried to make her voice sound casual.

"I'm sorry Mrs Floyd. There's a board meeting today and he won't be free until this afternoon."

"Oh, that's odd I thought the meeting was next week." Miriam managed to sound puzzled.

"It was brought forward because he's in Switzerland at a retail conference; he's giving the keynote speech."

"Of course," Miriam sighed. "I'd forgotten, I must put it on the calendar, he's away for two days isn't he?"

"No Mrs Floyd he flies out next Tuesday morning and doesn't come back until Sunday afternoon. Did you want to leave a message?"

"Oh, it's nothing important but you could say that I called and perhaps he would let me know if he's going to be late tonight. We've got neighbours round for drinks at 6.30. I expect he's forgotten."

Janet laughed. "Will do Mrs Floyd."

Miriam put the phone down and smiled. The call had only been necessary to confirm that Vincent was definitely out of the country next week. She picked up the phone again and dialled Andy's mobile.

He answered almost at once. "Hello darling, what a surprise, I didn't expect to hear from you."

"I just wanted you to know that I'm looking forward to our little trip next week. Vincent will definitely be in Switzerland from Tuesday to Sunday. Do you know, I can really almost feel the sun on my back?"

"I'll book us seats in business on an overnight Emirates flight, there's one that leaves at eleven forty that gets us to Dubai the next day in time for breakfast. What does he think you're doing?"

"Oh don't worry I'll think of something - that is if he even bothers to ask. I'll get a taxi to Heathrow and meet you at Terminal 3 by the information desk. I'll aim to get there about nine thirty"

"Get there about nine o'clock and we can have a drink and a snack in the club lounge. You know, get in the mood before we take off. Look, I must go I've got stuffy old Don coming to lecture me on marketing expenses; he'll be here any minute. I can hardly wait to see you again. By the way don't forget your passport."

"Don't be too impatient Andy darling," Miriam lowered her voice and added in a sultry tone, "Do I need anything else or just my passport?"

"Just bring yourself and a bikini." Andy rang off, his laugh echoing in her ears.

***

They reclined lazily in their business class seats aboard the Airbus A380 Emirates flight EK006 from Heathrow to Dubai. Whilst the economy passengers were finding their seats and pushing luggage into the overhead lockers Andy and Miriam sipped on cold champagne.

Andy had booked a three-night stay in one of the best hotels in Dubai. The Royal Palace had its own beach, a kilometre of fine, pale golden sand washed gently by the tepid waters of the Arabian Gulf. With the cost of the business class flights and the exclusive Palace Suite he had booked at almost four thousand pounds for the three nights, Andy had used up all of the money he had won on the Uttoxeter race and a bit more besides. Thinking of money his mind turned to Don Markham and his nagging on expenditure. Better forget that, he thought, all the more reason to get his money's worth and make Miriam earn the trip.

"You'll just love the Royal Palace." Andy squeezed Miriam's hand. "The flight gets in just around eight thirty in the morning and by the time we've checked in and had some breakfast it'll be just right to lie by the pool."

"Unless you've got something else in mind." Miriam blew him a kiss, her lips glossy with crimson lipstick, pouting and sensual.

"Plenty of time for that, we need a bit of sunshine first. Recharge those batteries."

They relaxed with more champagne as the cabin crew readied the plane for take-off. Their club seats in the reclined position, they both dozed throughout most of the seven-hour flight feeling the effects of the two bottles of champagne and the late hour.

As business class passengers they were among the first to leave the aircraft once the air bridge had been manoeuvred into place and the doors opened. They only had hand luggage and quickly passed through customs and into the arrival hall. Andy spotted a chauffeur, resplendent in a dark mauve uniform edged with gold piping, holding a placard that read ROYAL PALACE HOTEL the words in the same colour mauve. They walked toward him.

"Andy Clewer are you waiting for us?" He put their bags down onto the floor.

The chauffeur bowed slightly. "Welcome madam and sir. Let me take your bags." Picking up the bags he smiled at them. "Please follow me." He guided them across the concourse and outside to where a luxury limousine gleamed in the sunlight. The bodywork, emblazoned with the hotel's logo, shimmered in the heat of the early morning. He placed their bags in the boot and they settled back in the air conditioned luxury of the stretched BMW's black leather upholstery.

The drive from the airport took them round the edge of Dubai city down wide boulevards and dual carriageways and onto the Jumeriah Beach Road that ran parallel with the Gulf. Most of the buildings they passed were new, many of them eight, nine or more, stories tall. As they were driving past, Andy pointed out a building, shaped like the sail of an Arab dhow. Just off the beach it dominated the skyline and was built on an island reached by a short causeway.

"Look darling." He pointed through the tinted windows. "That's the Burj al Arab, one of the most expensive hotels in the world."

"Oh so you're taking me to a cheap hotel." Miriam pulled a face at him. "That makes me feel good."

"Not cheap my angel, less expensive. Just wait until you see the Royal Palace."

They passed one of the many palaces belonging to the ruling family. Set on a private stretch of beach and surrounded by high walls over which swaying palm trees towered.

"We're nearly there," Andy slipped his arm round her shoulders. "See there's a gate house, we turn in here."

As the BMW approached the gate house, white painted with a thatched roof of palm leaves, a man stepped out. Recognising the hotel's limousine he raised the barrier that guarded the entrance to the drive and stood saluting the passengers.

Waving to him Miriam laughed. "Arriving in style they must think we're royalty - I like it."

The car glided to a halt outside the private entrance to the Gold Club reception where an attentive doorman jumped forward to open the car door. As they stepped out the heat of the desert hit them and almost immediately beads of sweat started to trickle down their faces.

"This way madam and sir." The man, dressed in a tunic and wearing a turban and curly-toed shoes, bowed as he opened the sliding doors into the spacious high ceilinged reception area. Brightly coloured shrubs and fully grown palm trees rooted in huge earthenware pots adorned the centre of the floor with rug covered sofas placed discretely round the walls.

"Wow, Andy this is some place." Miriam gazed round marvelling at the sumptuous surroundings.

Taking her arm Andy guided her toward the reception desk. "It's pretty special, I told you so," he agreed.

With calm efficiency and politeness they were offered a cool drink, checked in and when their drinks were finished, were asked if they would like to go to their suite. They were led down corridors, thickly carpeted, the walls hung with gold framed pictures. Doors to the Gold Club rooms were positioned on one side of the corridor only, the rooms behind facing out toward the gardens, the beach and the Gulf. At intervals, set into the walls, were niches where fountains trickled water down moss covered stones and small rocks. Ferns grew between the stones and with subdued back lighting the effect was stunning.

They reached their suite and were exploring the balcony when a discreet knock at the door announced the arrival of their luggage. Tipping the man that had brought their bags Andy closed the door.

Within minutes it seemed they had unpacked and were slipping out of their clothes. Miriam shrugged her lithe body into a coral coloured bikini with a halter top whilst Andy pulled on a pair of light cotton swimming shorts.

"Managed to keep your hands off me then", Andy murmured caressing Miriam's neck and shoulders.

"M'mm, that's nice but have you seen the beach, and that swimming pool looks so inviting." She stretched and stood up. "Come on then, slip on your robe and we'll go and explore." She took the bath robes from the bathroom and threw one to Andy.

They took the lift to the ground floor and once again felt the blast of heat as they walked out into the gardens where a brilliant green lawn, studded with palm trees and flowering shrubs surrounded the pool.

They followed the paved pathway that headed in the direction of the pool and open air restaurant on the edge of the beach.

"I'll get us a couple of towels." Andy walked over to the thatched cabin where he collected enormous thick beach towels. "As we're in a Gold Club room we get a gazebo by the pool and our own reserved sun loungers."

He took her hand and they wandered along a path bordered by scented oleander and tall palm trees. "Here we are, two hundred and seven, that's ours."

They were glad to get into the shade of the awning. Slipping off her robe Miriam spread her towel out over one of the striped cushions that covered the slatted wooden loungers. Stretching out like a cat she let out a sigh of contentment. "Oh this is perfect."

Carrying a silver tray a man appeared and waited discreetly until Andy waved him forward.

"Good morning," he smiled, his teeth a brilliant white against his dark skin. "My name is Raff and I am here to look after you. Can I get you anything?"

Andy looked down at Miriam. "How about a beer to cool us down?" Without waiting for her reply he ordered two beers and sat down on the edge of his lounger.

"I'm going for a quick dip." He slipped off his robe and sandals and stepped out of the shade.

"Bloody hell!" He jumped back under the awning. "This paving's red hot. We'll have to wear our sandals." He reached down and taking her hands pulled her to her feet.

Slipping on their sandals they walked hand in hand across the hot paving stones to the broad expanse of steps that led down into the turquoise waters of the pool. The pool, shaped roughly like an octagon but for the fact that the edges followed a soft curve rather than sharp angles, must have covered an area of at least 300 square metres. Jutting out of the water were 4 small islands, stone edged pinnacles, and home to several more palm trees that were hung with bunches of dark brown dates.

It felt like heaven after the sun's fiery rays to lower their bodies into the water that had been cooled by the hotel's refrigeration plant. They floated on their backs and just drifted, eyes closed against the glare of the sun. Then they stood, waist deep in the water and watched other people swimming. When the heat got too much they would dip under the water, emerging cooled and refreshed.

"That's enough of this lazing around. I'll race you to that island in the middle." Miriam had already started to swim.

"Hey come back that's cheating." Andy pushed off from the side and with a powerful front crawl quickly caught her. He grabbed hold of her leg and pulled her under.

Letting himself slide under as well he pulled her toward him and put his arms around her, kissing her on the lips. They surfaced laughing and splashing like two children. Miriam flicked water at Andy.

"Don't start something you can't stop," he laughed and glanced toward their gazebo. "Besides it looks like the beer's arrived."

Miriam moved close to him and pressed her body against his. "Beer first and if you're a good boy a special treat." She moved her hips as she thrust toward him.

His body responded as she continued to push her hips against him. "Why not treat first and beer later."

She pulled away from him laughing. "You'd better wait in this cold water for a minute or two. You can't come out like that or else you'll make all the girls jealous." Miriam swam with a lazy backstroke to the steps. Climbing out, she slipped into her sandals.

"It'd give them something to talk about." Andy called teasing her as he waded through the water after her.

There was a poolside bar that served light meals all day. The barbecue was alight and the tantalising smell of fish grilling over the hot charcoal made Miriam's mouth water. "I'm hungry," she called, "What about something to eat?"

Reaching the side Andy pulled himself up onto the edge of the pool. "I'll see what there is when we've had our beer."

With his arm round her waist they strolled back the gazebo. Their beers were sitting on the silver tray, the glasses beaded with condensation. Picking up both glasses Andy handed one to Miriam. "Here's to a special treat." The glasses chinked as they brought them together.

"I'll drink to that." Miriam winked and moistened her lips with her tongue. "Be an angel and put some of that sun tan lotion on my back."

Andy picked up the bottle and unscrewed the top. "Lie down on the lounger and I'll oil you all over."

Lying on her stomach Miriam reached her hands round to her back and undid the clasp of her bikini top. She slipped the halter strap over her neck and relaxed as Andy began to massage the lotion into her skin. He worked the oil across her shoulders. For several minutes his fingers moved in tiny circles gently probing and caressing.

"Ooh that feels sensational." Miriam arched her back and Andy slipped his hands round her waist to her stomach and upwards to smooth oil onto her breasts. He felt her nipples harden in response to his touch.

"I don't think I can wait any longer for that treat." He pulled on his robe. "Here put this on." He slipped her robe round her shoulders.

Laughing she sat up and tied the robe round her waist. "Come on then." He took her hand and they almost ran back to the coolness of the hotel and the sanctuary of their room.

They made love with a desperate frenzy each trying to satisfy the other. Within minutes they had climaxed and lay in each other's arms.

"That was sensational." Andy nibbled at Miriam's ear. "You've worn me out."

Miriam could only manage to moan softly as she snuggled against him and as if orchestrated, their eyes closed and the room was filled with the sound of steady breathing.

Andy woke with a start. "We must have drifted to sleep. Do you realise its past lunchtime." He nudged Miriam.

"Let's have some lunch sent up here," he sat up and reached for the phone. "Salade Nicoise suit you?"

He ordered from room service and wondered if they had time to make love again before lunch arrived. He didn't have time to wonder for too long as Miriam eased herself down the bed and began kissing his stomach gradually moving down until she reached her destination.

They sat and ate lunch on the balcony and talked about nothing in particular.

***

It was 8.00 pm Swiss time on Thursday evening when Vincent got the call from Janet back in the office. A fire had started in the distribution warehouse and several of the staff had been overcome by smoke and were in hospital.

"Check the flights and book me on the earliest possible," he told her. "Get me picked up from Heathrow I want to see for myself. I'll also go to the hospital."

"I've already got you a seat on a British Airways flight leaving Geneva at 7.30 tomorrow morning as you have missed tonight's flight. It gets in to Heathrow at 8.20 so all being well you should be at the warehouse by mid-morning."

"Good. Get me any information you can on the extent of the damage, disruption to deliveries and whatever else. Oh and Janet get the details on those in hospital. A bit of background, family and so on. Have it in the car for me." Vincent hung up and went to find the conference organisers to make his apologies. At least he'd delivered his speech the day before.

His flight arrived on time and he was met by Colin, his driver, as he entered the arrivals hall. Together they paced quickly through the crowds to the exit where Vincent's Jaguar was parked on a double yellow line with the hazard lights flashing.

Colin opened the car door and Vincent settled into the front passenger seat. "You were taking a chance leaving the car here, it could have been clamped or towed away." Vincent snapped. "Where's the information from Janet?"

Opening the car boot Colin took out a small briefcase. Slamming the boot he hurried round to the driver's door and opening it got in. He passed the briefcase over and started the car.

The warehouse was situated at Welwyn Garden City. The drive took about an hour and throughout Vincent was either studying the sheath of papers contained in the briefcase or on his mobile phone talking to the warehouse manager, Janet or the operations director. By the time they arrived he had a pretty good idea of events and a strategy in place so as to ensure supplies to the stores were not disrupted.

He spent half an hour going through the contingency plans and another half hour walking round the warehouse. The fire had started in the plant room where the refrigeration and air-conditioning motors where housed. It appeared that someone had dumped rubbish, cardboard and some old rags, right against the motors. The motors had overheated and set fire to some of the rags that were impregnated with oil. The resulting pungent black smoke had permeated through the warehouse damaging stock and causing some of the warehouse operatives to inhale the sooty air.

By early afternoon he was sitting in a ward at the Queen Elizabeth II hospital. He spent five or six minutes at each bedside. In all 10 people had been rushed to the hospital but only 7 had been admitted. He assured them that they would be looked after and that they were not to worry they'd be kept on full pay until they were fit to return to work.

He checked with the doctor who had examined each of the patients and was reassured that, in his opinion, there would be no lasting effects and that they would probably be discharged in a day or two.

It was as he walked back to the car that he realised that he hadn't eaten anything but what passed for a light breakfast on the plane.

As they drove round the M25 toward the A3 and home he thought about phoning Miriam to let her know he was back.

"Oh bugger," he said aloud causing Colin to glance at him. He remembered she said that she would go and spend a few days with Suzanne at Crondall.

The traffic was heavy that evening. A lorry had broken down on the slip road leading onto the M3 and the tailback was five miles long and still building.

"Get us off here Colin, I'm starving. I'll treat you to supper and by the time we've finished the traffic will have cleared."

Colin thought for a moment. "I'll come off at the next junction. There's a good fish restaurant in Egham."

"That's fine. I've eaten there, Andy Clewer recommended it. I could eat a whale I'm starving."

As it was still early in the evening and there weren't many other diners. They were shown to a corner table near the back. Scarcely looking at the menu Vincent ordered grilled Dover sole, a salad and a half bottle Chilean viognier. Colin chose a pan fried sea bass with roasted vegetables and a bottle of Perrier water.

"Cosy little table this." Vincent snorted. "Sort of place Clewer would bring one of his lady friends."

The journey home didn't take long. The lorry had been removed, the tailback dispersed and the traffic was now quite light.

"Pick me up about nine on Monday morning." Vincent got out of the car. "I'll be in the office all day and drive myself home. Have the rest of the day off; take that wife of yours out somewhere."

Colin was delighted. "See you at nine on Monday, and thanks Mr Floyd." The car pulled away from the kerb and Vincent turned toward the front door and a house in darkness.

Throwing his bag on the floor inside the door he shrugged out of his jacket and walking into the lounge, switched on a table lamp that bathed the room with a warm glow.

He poured himself a generous slug of malt whisky from the cut glass decanter into one of the matching tumblers and was about to sit down when the phone rang. Glancing at his watch he frowned. It was almost 7.30. "Hello," he answered tiredly.

"Vincent, hi, sorry to bother you is Miriam there?"

He sat down. The voice was familiar yet he couldn't place it. "That's OK; I've only just got home. Who's that?"

"Are you sure you haven't been drinking, surely you recognise me, it's Suzanne."

"Suzanne. Is this a wind up?" He ran his hand through his hair. "I thought Miriam was with you."

"Is she out then? Suzanne breathed out with a snort that made Vincent move the receiver away from his ear. "Too late for shopping, she must have got a fancy man."

"That's not funny Suzanne." Vincent paused. "I should be in Switzerland right now but there was a problem, a fire, and I came back early. I expect she's gone to the pictures or something. I'll get her to call you in the morning."

"That's great; I want to ask her if she can come down for a few days. See you soon." She rang off leaving Vincent puzzled. If Miriam wasn't there where was she?

Picking up the phone he dialled her mobile only to be told that the phone he was calling was switched off.

He took a sip from the tumbler. The fiery drink burned in his throat. He swallowed but was unable to enjoy the taste of his favourite whisky. Perhaps another glass might help!

Saturday morning he was up late, too much whisky he thought to himself as he made a pot of coffee and stuck two slices of bread into the toaster. He tried Miriam's mobile again but got the same message as last night.

Wandering into the hall he picked up the paper before going back to the kitchen when he heard the toast pop up.

Settling down to toast and coffee he scanned through the pages until he reached the sports section. Great, Richmond were at home that afternoon so he could watch a good game of rugby, have a couple of beers in the club house and then home to see if his missing wife had returned.

Chapter 10

Miriam was alarmed to see lights on in the lounge as she let herself into the house. The flight from Dubai had landed 30 minutes late at just before 7.00pm and with hand luggage they were through immigration and customs and out into the arrivals hall in less than 20 minutes. A frustrating 10 minute wait in the queue for a taxi before Andy waved her off. The journey at that time on a Saturday evening to Richmond only took 25 minutes so she was home by nearly 8 o'clock.

"Where the hell have you been?" Vincent's gruff voice came from the lounge making her jump.

"Hello darling I didn't expect you until tomorrow evening," Miriam closed the front door relieved that he couldn't see her. "I'll just take these bits upstairs and be down in a jiffy"

She ran upstairs and into the dressing room. With almost frantic haste she pulled clothes out of her overnight bag and stuffed them into the laundry basket. Reaching up she put the now empty bag on top of her wardrobe. Smoothing down her skirt she stood to look at her reflection in the long wardrobe mirror. Satisfied with her appearance she went down stairs.

Sitting down in an armchair she was surprised to see him wearing blue corduroy trousers with his wax jacket covering a thick woollen pullover and casual blue checked shirt.

"Do you always dress like that for your flight home from Geneva?" Her flippant tone made him frown.

Pulling off his coat he threw it onto a chair. "Fix me a G and T, will you? I've been to the rugby stayed and had a couple of jars in the club house and only just got in myself." He turned to look at her. "By the way, I came home yesterday as you would have known if you'd been here. They had a fire at the distribution centre. Where were you anyway? Not at Suzanne's, she phoned for you."

Standing up quickly, Miriam hid her confusion by walking toward the drinks cabinet. "Get some ice will you there's a dear." She took out the bottle of Gordon's Gin. Her mind raced as she tried to come up with a plausible reason for being away.

Vincent raised his voice from the kitchen. "I thought you were spending a few days with her - Suzanne I mean." He walked back to the lounge with a small bowl of ice and some slices of fresh lime.

Taking the bowl from him Miriam dropped three pieces of ice and a slice of lime into the tumbler of gin. She topped it up with tonic water passing him the glass before making a drink for herself.

"Harriet phoned yesterday afternoon; a girl in my Pilates class. Said her husband had gone away and remembered that I had said you were away so why not have a girls' get-together. She invited some of the others from the class and we made a night of it."

Vincent took a gulp of his drink. "I said you'd call her, Suzanne I mean. What are we eating tonight?"

"Just you enjoy your drink. I'll give Suzanne a quick ring and then grill you a piece of steak with some salad, how's that?"

"Sounds good. I've got a bottle of Californian zinfandel I can open."

Miriam used the phone in the study away from Vincent's prying ears to call Suzanne. She told her the same story about Harriet and listened to the latest saga in the history of Suzanne's quest to lose weight. Arranging to meet later in the week she hung up.

It was as they were getting ready for bed later that night that Vincent's suspicions were aroused once again.

Miriam had slipped off her skirt and blouse and was taking off her bra when he noticed the colour of her skin. Where the strap of her bikini had gone over her shoulders and round her neck the skin was white. There was a marked contrast to where the hot desert sun had reddened her shoulders and back.

"You've been out in the sun." His voice was harsh with accusation. "How come you've got a sun tan?"

"Nonsense darling - you're imagining it." Miriam always wore a silk nightie in bed and she quickly slipped this over her head.

Striding across the room Vincent grabbed hold of her by the shoulders. He twisted her body round toward the dressing table where there was a light. He shook her. "What the hell's that then - it's sunburn."

"Vincent, let go. You're hurting me."

"Answer me. How come you get a suntan in October? It's practically winter."

Miriam pulled away from him. "Under Harriet's sun lamp, that's where."

"How come I've never heard of bloody Harriet until now?" Vincent shouted.

"It's not my fault that you don't listen when I talk about my friends." Miriam sniffed and rubbed her shoulders. "All you think about is work."

"That's right blame me." Vincent grabbed his dressing gown off the back of the door. "I'm going to sleep in the other bedroom. I don't want to spoil your suntan." He jerked open the door and slammed it shut as he stalked out of the room.

He couldn't get to sleep. Thoughts chased through his mind. Nagging demons of mistrust. Had she told him about Harriet? He really couldn't remember. He put the light out, turned onto his side and tried to settle down.

About 25 minutes had passed and Vincent lay on his side, eyes closed but not quite asleep. He heard the door open. He could smell Miriam's perfume before he felt the bed dip slightly as she slid under the duvet and lay next to him. She moved up to curve her body to the contours of his back.

"Darling." She breathed the word into his ear. "I don't like it when we argue." Her arm went round his waist and her fingers caressed tiny patterns on his stomach.

He tried to ignore her but his body was already responding to the light touch. She slid her hand down into the front of his pyjamas and her probing hand gripped him firmly.

He turned to face her. A table lamp on the landing shed a warm glow of light into the room and he could see that she was naked. Before he was able to speak her lips pressed down onto his. Her hand began to move up and down, gently at first but as she sensed his arousal getting more urgent, she tightened her hold.

She moved her lips round to his ear. "I do love you and I really want you."

She lay back and pulled him toward her. Scrambling out of his pyjama trousers Vincent rolled over. He manoeuvred himself between her legs.

Miriam filled her thoughts with Andy and how it had been when they made love in Dubai as Vincent made stabbing thrusts. Within moments he groaned and flopped back onto the bed turning onto his side. She knew it would only be a matter of a few minutes before he was asleep.

She kissed him on his back. "Goodnight darling I'm so glad we've made up."

***

Out on the golf course the next morning Vincent was playing in a foursome. They were walking toward the tenth to tee off, arguing about the merits of the euro and its effect on the European economy.

"Damn glad my business deals in the good old pound." Vincent took his driver and lined up behind the ball. Glancing up he studied the flag nearly 300 yards away. He gripped the driver firmly and lowered his head to focus his attention on the ball. Back came the head of the club and with a defiant swing it whipped through the air to connect with the ball in a satisfying thwack.

Vincent raised his head to see the ball lofted skyward. It landed bounced and rolled off the edge of the fairway seemingly under a gorse bush.

"Bugger." Vincent thrust the driver back into the bag. "Looks more like the Grand National, bloody bushes all over the place like fences on a racecourse."

His partner, a local solicitor, sympathised. "Talking of racecourses saw your wife the other day on the winner's podium - at Uttoxeter I think it was. Not a golf ball in sight."

"Are you sure it was Miriam?" They pulled their golf carts forward and started to walk up the fairway.

"Absolutely certain, old boy. I had to meet a client that afternoon so I videoed the race." The solicitor smiled. "I backed the favourite and it got beaten by that horse of your pal, Andy Clewer."

"Oh yes." Vincent forced a smile. "Of course, Uttoxeter." His game, never brilliant at the best of times went completely to pieces as his mind buzzed with the thought of Miriam lying to him. As they walked into the club house the others ribbed him about losing a ball on each of the last two holes.

His partner pulled off his golf shoes. "Come and drown your sorrows, I'll even buy you a large one you look so miserable. It's only a game you know."

Unusually for him, he declined a drink after the game feeling the need to be on his own and to think things through. "Got people for Sunday lunch. Must dash – next week same time?"

Not really waiting for a reply Vincent changed his shoes and strode to his car. Getting in he just sat there. The thoughts marched into his head without him trying - Uttoxeter races with Andy, him away and she going to a friends when she should have been with Andy's wife. Why Andy's wife? Of course he was away as well. Cosy arrangement, they'd been somewhere hot that's why the suntan. He could see the two of them on a beach, his hands all over her. In bed together.

He tried to stop the thoughts but it wasn't that easy. He imagined Andy thrusting into her as he had done last night. Who gave her the most satisfaction? He banged his hands onto the steering wheel – the rage building inside.

"She's gone too far this time." He said aloud. "And as for that bastard Clewer." He left the threat hanging in the air. Something niggled in the back of his mind. Uttoxeter races – that was it. He'd met Don that evening. Don who said he wanted to do a deal with information he had on Andy. Well maybe it was time to talk to Don again.

'If that's the game she wants to play,' he thought as emotion kicked in, 'she can have him. But I'll take him for every penny he's got.' His mind made up Vincent decided he needed the drink he'd turned down.

Using the car phone he rang Miriam at home. "I'm having lunch at the golf club then I've got a bit of business so I might be late." His lips twisted in a wicked grin. "Don't wait up for me my angel."

"Oh darling, I was hoping we might have supper together. Can't you do business in the week?"

"No something's come up got to get it sorted right away. You'll probably be asleep by the time I get in so I'll see you in the morning." He rang off, got out of the car and sauntered into the club bar.

"Got the wrong week, lunch next week – here let me buy this round." He glanced toward the solicitor. "I wouldn't mind borrowing that video, see how Clewer's horse ran."

Chapter 11

It was just after the Monday morning sales meeting when Debbie buzzed through to tell Andy that Adrian was on the phone.

Pressing the hands-free button Andy stretched out in his black leather chair. Pulling open one of the lower drawers in the desk he rested his feet and put his hands behind his head.

"Adrian, how are things? All ready for the big one - what eleven days from now?" He smiled at the thought of being a winning owner of one of the biggest races.

"Andy, that's why I'm calling. Bad news I'm afraid." Adrian Fordham's voice boomed from the loud speaker on the telephone.

Moving quickly Andy snatched up the handset cutting off the loud speaker. "What do you mean, not a problem I hope?"

"AW injured himself on the gallops this morning. He's walking lame. He must have overreached and kicked into himself."

"Bloody hell, what about the race? I'm out on a limb with the bookies." The colour drained from his face as he thought of the bet he'd laid on AW to win. "He will win won't he?

"Andy I'm not even sure that he'll run never mind win. We've got to give him a few days off and reduce the swelling in his near foreleg. Any decision about him running won't be made until then at the earliest. I'm just putting you in the picture."

"Adrian, who else knows about this?"

"Well only the lads in the yard and of course the vet."

"Keep everything under wraps. Make sure none of the lads talk. I'll get out to see you probably tomorrow. Adrian, I'm in deep shit if that horse doesn't win." Putting down the phone Andy sat staring at the lake outside his office window.

There was a calculator and an A4 pad on the desk. Using his gold Mont Blanc pen he made a list of the money he owed. He totalled up the column of figures.

"Bloody hell." His eyes widened as for the first time he realised the extent of his debts. The figure that stared back at him seemed in stark relief to the whiteness of the paper.

If the horse didn't win he knew it would be hard to reel in those debts. His elbows rested on the desk, his head bent into his hands. He owed almost £900,000. Even if Alternative Ways won, the prize money and his winnings would only be a drop in the ocean. But to Andy at that moment a drop in the ocean would give him time, time that he now began to realise he desperately needed.

There was no way he could get out of the bet he'd laid. His £5,000 credit limit, used up to the hilt, was £5,000 pounds he didn't have. If the horse didn't run or ran and didn't win then he would have to pay up. It was almost too much to bear the thought of the horse losing.

Andy sat up. Of course. Back the horse to loose and he'd clean up. The bookies weren't to know that the horse wasn't fully fit. The more he thought about the more certain he was that this was the way to make a lot of money. Lay the red hot favourite to lose with the betting exchange.

Already he felt better. "Debbie – in here now and bring the diary."

"What's the week like, I need a day out?" He asked as Debbie brought in the diary and a cup of coffee for Andy.

"There's the meeting with Don tomorrow, the return visit of the Swedish distributors in the afternoon. Board meeting Wednesday, we could probably clear Thursday.

"See if you can move Don to Thursday. I'll take Tuesday morning off and be back for the meeting with the Swedes. I'll be at the stables if you need me. And Debbie – don't take no for an answer from Don."

The phone on Debbie's desk began ringing. Leaning over to reach Andy's phone she picked up the call.

"Andy Clewer's office." She smiled at Andy. "Just one moment Mr Floyd, I'll see if he's in his office." She pressed the secrecy button. "Vincent Floyd, says he needs a quick word."

Andy took the receiver from her and pressed the button again. "Vincent, how are you?" He jerked his head toward the door and put his hand over the mouthpiece. "Get onto Don and sort out that meeting, there's a good girl."

Hand off the mouthpiece. "Sorry Vincent, yes the horse won at Uttoxeter, didn't know you were interested in horseracing. Tell you what, get your money on him for the big race at Cheltenham."

He paused as his ego took over at the thought of playing the big owner. "Why don't you come to see the race first hand? Better still bring Miriam - Suzanne loves the big race meetings I'm sure Miriam will as well." As usual Andy had taken a box at Cheltenham. "Come as my guests it'd be good to see Miriam again. George Nicol and his wife are coming it should be a great day."

Vincent rang off with the promise that he'd check his diary and get back.

***

Don Markham was cursing Andy. He'd been forced to rearrange his diary and all because Andy wanted to see his bloody horse. The beeping of his phone only served to increase the sense of rage he was feeling.

"Yes," he barked into the receiver.

"Don, its Vincent Floyd, don't bite my head off, can you talk?"

"Vincent, sorry. Yes I can talk. Just cursing our mutual friend."

"You remember our meeting the other night. Well, perhaps I was a little bit hasty." Vincent paused. "Can we start that discussion again?"

Don sat up. "Yes of course. Do you have a date in mind?"

Vincent looked at his computer monitor and flicked onto his diary page. "Soon as you like. Dinner tonight if you can make it. My treat this time."

Don didn't need to check his diary. He was due to play squash that evening, but this was far more important. "No problem. Where do you suggest?"

Vincent scratched his cheek. "Somewhere discreet. There's a pub on the towpath just down by the bridge over the river in Kingston. Can't remember the name."

Don interrupted him. "The Boatman - I know it. 7 o'clock suit?"

***

Vincent made sure he got to the pub before Don. The vodka and ice drinkers hadn't yet turned out and the 'one after work' office workers had all but gone on their way home. There were only a handful of people and no one sitting near the table Vincent had chosen.

Don arrived and the two men shook hands. "I'll get you a drink. Gin and tonic?" Vincent moved toward the bar.

"I think I'll have a pint of lager, Stella if they have." Don picked up the menu that was wedged between the salt and pepper pots on the table.

In a few minutes Vincent sat down with two pint glasses putting one on the table in front of Don.

He waved the menu at Vincent. "Dinner won't cost you much, I should have insisted on at least a restaurant with table cloths."

"I've even ordered for you." Vincent smiled. "Jacket potato with coleslaw and salad." He leaned forward. "I didn't arrange to meet you for the food. I want you to tell me about Clewer and how we can screw him."

"Whoa." Don frowned. "That's a turnaround from last time we spoke. Why the sudden change of heart?"

"Let's say that I've seen a video and he's taken me for a ride. I want to get my own back. Leave it at that Don and help me shaft the bastard."

"Ok, fair enough but what do I get out of this?" Don smiled. "You know I want a share of the business, so how does that work?"

Vincent raised his eyebrows. "What you've always wanted – a piece of the equity and me as your fellow shareholder."

The jacket potatoes arrived and stood cooling and congealing into solid lumps as the two men talked. Don had brought with him the four ring binder that contained the details of Andy's money siphoning activities. The binder compiled over the years using the master finance files.

As the evening wore on the two men examined and discussed the ways in which Andy had manoeuvred and manipulated the marketing account to satisfy his ever increasing need for money to settle his gambling debts. Going through the records that Don had gathered Vincent was amazed at the extravagant expenditure when it came to entertaining.

Don had a notebook and from time to time would scribble a figure or a few words, filling up five pages by the time they had finished putting together a plan. One that would see him as a major shareholder in Clewer Alternatives and Vincent Floyd getting his revenge.

A waitress had long ago removed their untouched plates of food but they had eased their hunger with a packet of crisps and another pint of lager each.

"I'm meeting with him on Thursday." Don took a sip from his glass. "Is that too soon for you? I mean half a million pounds in cash is a lot of money to raise in a short space of time?"

"Just perfect - it'll give me time to draw up the papers." Vincent nodded. "Don't you worry about the cash side of things. I set up a trust fund about 10 years ago to provide for my old age. I can pull half a million out and get a bankers draft organised. So long as the collateral is good there won't be a problem." He paused. "Are you sure he'll go for this?"

"I'm telling you he's desperate. If he thinks he can get his hands on that kind of money he'd sell his wife."

"No thanks Don." Vincent gave a lop-sided smile. "I've got enough problems with the one I've got."

As he sat in the taxi taking him back home to Richmond, Vincent let his mind roam. Yes he felt bitter about the way Miriam had behaved but he was not sure that he really wanted to go through life without her. She was lively and vivacious to his seriousness and plodding determination. She was good for him he had no doubt about that. Perhaps he was too serious and plodding.

"Twelve pound sixty." The taxi driver had pulled back the sliding glass partition that separated them and was looking at Vincent. "We're here Guv."

Vincent had been so deep in thought that he hadn't realised that they had arrived outside the house in Richmond. "Oh, yes." He pulled out his wallet and fished out a ten and a five pound note. "Here, keep the change."

"Thanks Guv, goodnight." The taxi clattered away from the kerb leaving behind a haze of diesel fumes. Sighing Vincent fished out his keys and let himself in through the front door.

Chapter 12

The banging of the wardrobe door woke Suzanne from a deep sleep and a dream where she was stepping out on the catwalk of a Paris fashion show. She was wearing an evening gown designed by Donatella Versace that showed off her hour glass size 10 figure. The audience were going wild in a frenzy of applause.

"What's going on?" She rolled over. With a jolt she realised the size 10 figure had been a dream as the duvet pulled at her ample legs. The light was on in the bedroom and she looked with bleary eyes at the clock on the bedside table. "It's not even 7 o'clock, why are you up so early?"

"Go back to sleep." Andy pushed a gold cuff link into the buttonhole of his shirt sleeve. "I'm going to the stables this morning, didn't I tell you?"

Suzanne pushed herself up in bed and arranged the pillow against the headboard. "You never tell me anything nowadays."

Andy pulled a dark maroon tie spotted with tiny bright yellow flowers from the rack on the wardrobe door. "Well I'm telling you now. I'll get some breakfast at the yard so don't bother getting up." He glanced in the mirror as he smoothed his collar down over the knot he had tied. "I may be late back."

Suzanne sniffed. "So what's new? I'm out to lunch so I won't be needing dinner tonight you'd better feed yourself."

He slipped on his jacket. "Suits me. I'll eat out tonight." Blowing her a kiss he walked out of the bedroom and down the stairs.

"See you later." Before stepping out into the chill of the October morning he activated the doors to the double garage.

Pulling the front door shut he crunched his way across the gravelled turning circle getting the keys to the Aston Martin from his pocket. He pressed the remote on the key and heard the locks undo on the car.

Sitting in the driver's seat he started the engine and reversed the car out. With gravel spurting from beneath the rear wheels he gunned the engine and the car shot forward and down the drive to the road.

Behind him the garage doors moved silently down closing with a gentle thump.

At that time of the morning the M25 was still flowing fairly freely and his trip from Crondall round to the M4 was completed swiftly. The traffic on the M4 heading toward London was just starting to build up around Reading as Andy moved at a steady 80 miles an hour in the opposite direction.

It was just after eight am when he turned into the stable yard, parked beside the office and switched off the engine. Apart from a couple of girls mucking out loose boxes and the odd equine head peering over stable doors, the yard was deserted. No sign of Adrian or his Land Rover.

Andy sat for a few moments thinking about the conversation he was going to have with Adrian. Adrian would argue. After all his job was to get horses ready to win – not to lose.

Getting out of the car he strode through the yard until he reached AW's box. The horse had his back to him but turned his head at the sound of Andy's footsteps crunching on the flagstone path. With a faint snicker Alternative Ways moved toward the door. Andy looked anxiously down at the horse's legs in an effort to see the damage that had kept the horse in his box.

"Hello feller." He rubbed the horse's nose. "Been in the wars have we? Still you're favourite for the big one and we're going to clean up when you don't win." The horse pushed at Andy's hand searching for a mint his soft lips snaffling at Andy's palm. "Mints later when I've spoken to the Boss." With a final rub of the horse's nose he turned and walked across the yard back toward the office. He waved a hand in greeting to the two girls as he passed them pushing their wheelbarrows full of horse dung and the shredded paper that was used as bedding for the horses.

He went into the office. "Anyone at home?" His voice resounded in the empty room but a muffled shout came from within the kitchen behind.

The door to the kitchen opened and Mary peered at him. "Hello Mr Andy. Young Adrian said you might be in today so I was just cooking you a bit of breakfast in case. They're all up at the gallops with the second lot. You just sit down and I'll dish yours up before they come back."

Without waiting she turned back into the kitchen and Andy could hear the door to the AGA being opened. He followed her through and sat at the table. Minutes later he had a plate of steaming sausages and bacon in front of him and suddenly felt very hungry. A wry smile played on his lips as a stray thought popped into his mind - the condemned man ate a hearty meal.

Mary juggled with two frying pans, cooking a mountain of bacon, fried bread and more sausages. As each batch was cooked she piled them onto plates which she put into the AGA's top oven to keep warm. Through the clatter of plates Andy could hear the sound of the Land Rover's engine as Adrian drove into the yard.

This is it he thought as he jumped up from his chair. Passing through the office he met Adrian as he got out of the driver's door. Jonny, the assistant trainer, got out of the passenger side.

Andy shook Adrian's hand and waved acknowledgement to Jonny. "We need to talk."

Jonny nodded. "I'll see to the next lot and get Aunt Sally ready to go to Fontwell. The box should be here any time now. See you later Mr Clewer." He turned and hurried away just as the horses came into the yard from the gallops.

"Can we talk somewhere?" Looking round Andy watched as the stable staff went about their duties.

"Why don't we go and see your horse." Adrian led the way explaining as they walked how the horse had got injured. "I like to give horses a couple of pieces of fast work in the three weeks leading up to a race. AW had cantered once and was working well. A blasted pheasant put up from under the hedge about two thirds of the way up the gallops as he was doing his fast work. It didn't bother him but he jinked slightly and that's when I think he must have knocked into himself."

They arrived at AW's loose box and Adrian opened up the door. Pulling a bridle off a hook he slipped it over the horse's head. "Whoa big feller." He spoke softly to the horse as he buckled the bridle.

As he led the horse out into the yard, Andy could see the cut on the back of one of the horse's front legs. Adrian led the horse round and it was obvious he was favouring the leg slightly. With the horse standing still Adrian bent forward and ran his hand over the leg.

"Still a bit of heat in it but we give a cold poultice twice a day and that seems to be bringing the swelling down and reducing the heat."

Andy shrugged his shoulders. "The race is in less than two weeks won't he be OK by then?"

"Oh sure the leg should be OK by then. The swelling will have gone down and the cut healed but we won't be able to work him at all which means he won't be race fit."

"But you can still run him?"

"We could but it's a pretty competitive race and his fitness would let him down. I can't see that he would be fit enough to win."

Andy smiled. "But if he were still favourite and everyone else thought he was fit enough to win we could make a packet backing him to lose."

A look of horror appeared on Adrian's face. "Backing your own horse to lose; they won't let you do that. Besides I don't won't to run him if he's not fit. I know you'll lose the entry fee but that's peanuts to you."

"I'll get someone else to back him, someone I can trust." Andy's face was animated at the thought of pulling off a betting coup that, if he could get enough money together, would wipe the slate clean. "Look, you just make sure that not a word gets out about him being lame and get him to the races looking a picture – I'll do the rest. And Adrian, of course I'll cut you in. Should be a few thou in it."

"I'm not sure about this." Adrian scratched the side of his head. "I could be warned off if the Jockey Club thought I was running a horse to lose."

"But that's it isn't it?" Andy laughed. "You'd be running him to win, only he won't."

"You're right he needed another week of work to put him spot on." Adrian pulled a face. "He would have been the biggest winner the yard has ever had."

Andy punched him lightly on the arm. "At least we can salvage something from this. I don't mind telling you that I need to have a good winning bet. I've been a bit - shall we say - extravagant lately. Work with me on this Adrian, I'm going to raise enough money to back him to lose and with the winnings I'll be able to clear the slate and bung you say £10k."

"I could certainly use £10k – reduce my overdraft and make life a lot easier." Adrian pulled at his bottom lip as he weighed up the chances of being found out. "OK I'll run him and tell the lads that I think he's fit enough. But let me tell you Andy, if there's any sort of enquiry I know nothing about you backing him to lose. That's the deal."

"You won't regret it. We'll both do alright out of this. Right now I've got to get the money and get the bet placed with the exchanges." The horse moved from one leg to the other and snorted.

"You don't mind not winning do you?" Andy rubbed the horse's ears. "I'm off I'll be in touch."

Andy walked quickly across the yard to his car. He revved the engine and with a wave to Adrian swept out of the yard. As he drove down the lane he wrestled with the problem of getting enough money to make his bet worthwhile. He hadn't put Miriam's number into the car phone memory in case Suzanne should discover it so he pulled into the gateway to a field and punched in her home number. As the waited for the call to connect he glanced at his watch. Nearly 9 am. Good! Vincent would be out of the house by now so no awkward questions.

"Hello." Miriam's sleepy voice cut into his thoughts.

"Miriam it's me can you talk?"

"Andy, what time is it?" Miriam sat up in bed. "And yes we can talk Vincent left ages ago"

"Are you still in bed?" Andy imagined Miriam's supple figure stretched out under the duvet. "I need to meet up with you, today, in fact this morning. I need your help my darling, to make a lot of money."

Having arranged to meet Andy pulled a note book from the glove compartment. Pausing to think carefully he then started to write. When he'd finished he pulled the page from the book and stuffed it into his pocket.

They met in a coffee shop in Esher just after 11. Miriam was nursing a skinny latte and nibbling at a bread stick when Andy pushed open the door and stood looking round.

She waved the fingers of her left hand in greeting. "Over here."

He paced quickly across the floor bumping the chair of a middle aged lady having morning coffee with her friends.

"Sorry I'm late." He bent and kissed her on the cheek. "Hell of a job parking round here."

"A black coffee please." He turned and called to the girl behind the counter where the espresso machine was belching steam into a pot.

He moved a chair closer to Miriam and sat down. "I need you to put a bet on for me."

"If you think I'm going into some smelly betting shop to be leered at you can think again."

"Oh nothing like that. I need you to open an account with Leisure Industries. I'll put money in the account and all you do is place a bet using that money. Simple really."

"Simple really." She mimicked pulling a face. "And how do I go about this simple task?"

"Don't worry my sweet. You can open the account on line and I'll arrange to transfer money into your bank account. Then we, or rather you, after a couple of days make your bet."

Miriam scowled. "And I guess you tell me what to back, another of your sure-fire winners I suppose?"

"Oh yes. We'll make a deal at good odds and walk away with a lot of money. I mean a lot of money." Andy put his hand on Miriam's leg and squeezed gently. "We'll be able to do better than Dubai. How about Mustique or, his eyes opened wide as the thought hit him, "Neckar Island."

"You mean that lovely house with all those servants just for the two of us?" Miriam looked at him with wide eyes. Pressing his hand onto her leg and sliding it gently upwards. "Ooh yes please." Miriam whispered.

"First things first, my angel." Andy wriggled his fingers against her leg. "We need to get the account set up first. Does Vincent use the computer at home?"

"Vincent and computers don't go together. I don't think he even knows how to switch it on. Says he has people to do that for him. Little miss frigid knickers in the office. Chauvinist pig."

Andy pulled the note he had written earlier from his inside jacket pocket and smoothed it out onto the table. "It's all written down here. Just follow the instructions and the account will be opened."

"Log onto www.leisurebetexchange.co.uk." Miriam traced the words with her finger as she read them out. "Click onto new client registration and follow the prompts. Easy enough."

"You'll need to have your bank details handy as the bank account and your betting account feed each other. You make a bet and the money is taken from your bank account. You win and the winnings plus your original bet are transferred in. Can you set this up today?"

"My, my, you are anxious." Miriam teased. "I might be able to if I have time after I've been shopping."

His voice was harsh and low and his hand gripped her leg so tightly it started to feel numb. She tried to pull her leg away. "This is bloody important. I can't afford for this to go wrong. So don't mess me about. Can you do it today or not?" He emphasised every word with increased pressure on her leg seeming to stop the flow of blood to that part of her anatomy.

"You're hurting me." Her voice almost breaking. "Yes I'll do it the moment I get in. Please Andy my leg." She pulled at his hand. His fingers loosen their grip and the blood flowed once again.

"That's my girl." He moved his hand up her thigh anticipating the soft feel of her panties. Instead his fingers felt nothing at first but the smoothness of her skin.

"Shall I see if there's a room free at that motel down the road." His fingers caressed the silky hair between her legs. "After all you seem to have come ready for action." His voice thickened as he leant over and whispered in her ear. "Unless you want me to carry on right here."

"Damn you Andy Clewer." Miriam's voice was tight with emotion – her anger toward him losing the battle with her desire for him. "You squeeze my leg so hard that I'll have bruises. I should tell you to go to hell." She felt his fingers exploring. "But," she edged herself forward in her chair so that his fingers could feel how moist she was, "get that room and show me how you're going to make it up to me."

At home later that afternoon after she had showered Miriam slipped on a silk kimono and sat in front of the computer screen. Making the Internet connection, she logged onto Leisure Industries web site and followed the instructions to open a cash account on the betting exchange. An instant message came back.

> YOUR APPLICATION HAS BEEN SUCCESSFUL.
> YOUR ACCOUNT NUMBER AND PASSWORD WILL BE SENT
> TO YOU TODAY SEPARATELY BY FIRST CLASS POST.
> THE FIRST TIME YOU LOGON PLEASE CHANGE THE
> PASSWORD TO ONE OF YOUR OWN CHOICE.

She leaned back in the chair, the kimono slithering away to expose her legs. Looking down she could see the bruises left by Andy's fingers. "Better put some arnica on that," she said aloud gently touching the purple tinged marks on the inside of her thigh. "You really are a bastard Andy. Hurt a girl one minute and satisfy her the next. I wonder what you're really capable of." So unpredictable, she thought but maybe that's why she was drawn to him. She was more than a little frightened he was a strong man and he'd really hurt that morning.

Her thoughts wandered. Sex with Vincent was a non-event but with Andy, well it was electric, exciting and she was lifted to a dizzy height. She knew she was playing a risky game. She could lose Vincent and she was not sure she wanted to. Andy would drop her in an instant if he thought he could do better elsewhere. She resolved to have a rethink about their affair - she smiled - after Neckar Island that is.

Chapter 13

The Board meeting on Wednesday lasted most of the day. One item on the agenda toward the end of the afternoon was causing Andy untold concern. 'Overspend on Marketing' read the item, 'Finance Director's Report'. They had just taken tea and the opportunity for a natural break. It was the next point up for discussion as they returned to their seats. His anxiety increased as the Company Secretary brought their attention back to the Agenda.

Don looked round at his Board colleagues. "I've been monitoring the marketing account quite closely this year." He paused and glanced toward Andy. "It's true that we've a considerable overspend and I thought it appropriate that we made it a separate item on the agenda."

Andy felt his stomach lurch. Had Don discovered that he'd been settling his gambling debts with money from the marketing account? He leaned forward. His mouth felt dry, his tongue sticking to the roof of his mouth. "Don," he almost croaked.

"No, no Andy." Don shook his head. "I need everyone to know what you've been doing."

Andy knew that although he owned the company he was still bound by the rules of Companies House and other accounting and financial regulations that meant he couldn't just take money from the business. Besides which the Inland Revenue would very much like to know that he'd been taking tax free monies. And, anyway, he still had to account to the Board. They would have no option but to sack him and have him disbarred as a director. The thought of losing all he had built up terrified him. No more high life. No more horses or beautiful women to bed. No sleek cars like the Aston Martin.

He poured some iced mineral water into the crystal tumbler set beside his place at the head of the boardroom table. He fought to keep his hand from shaking and his heart was racing while he watched Don glance down at the papers in front of him.

"Yes the over-spend is attributable directly to Andy." Don shuffled the papers. "He has been working hard with the Swedes, wining and dining them and taking them to the races I'm sure." He paused and glanced round the table. "At yesterday's meeting all Andy's hard work paid off. They want to distribute our products throughout Norway and Denmark as well as Sweden and the deal we did with them should push our overall annual sales up by between 10 and 15%. The gross profit margin on the range they're selling averages around 35%. All thanks to Andy. I'd like to propose that we authorise the overspend retrospectively and record our thanks to our Chief Executive for securing a lucrative deal."

Doug Jackson, one of the non-exec directors seconded the proposal and Andy was able to bask in the collective thanks of the Board. He glanced across at Don who raised an eyebrow and gave him a slight smile.

Back in his office after the meeting Andy sat at his desk. It was nearly six o'clock and most people had gone home. He glanced up as he heard the door open.

"Spare me a minute Andy." Don lounged against the door frame. "I think we need to talk."

"Come in and close the door." Andy's mind raced as he tried to figure out what Don was up to. Could it be blackmail? He'll keep quiet in return for a chunk of the business. No it couldn't be that. If he'd been monitoring the accounts like he said he should have reported it months ago. No, he was implicated by not saying anything. Having rationalised it Andy felt better as he moved to the sofa and pointed to an easy chair beside the coffee table.

"Take a pew, Don. What's on your mind?" He grinned. "Thanks for heaping glory upon me today. I must admit I thought it a good deal with the Swedes."

"I won't beat about the bush." Don shrugged his shoulders as he sat down. "I know that you've got financial worries and that you've been helping yourself from the till. I don't just mean all that bollocks about the Swedes. I'm thinking more about the transfers to a bank account for Leisure Industries and...."

Andy held up his hand stopping him in mid-sentence. "If you're trying to blackmail me, Don, it won't work."

"I'm trying to help you and the company. I think you've forgotten that the auditors are due next month. It won't take them long to spot what's been going on and that will put us all in queer-street."

"OK. So what do you suggest?" Andy stood up and began pacing up and down the office. "I can't put any of the money back." He held his arms out wide. "I haven't got it anymore."

"Our meeting tomorrow." Without waiting for an answer Don carried on. "I'd like to bring Vincent Floyd in on our discussions."

"Oh, no way." Andy stopped in front of Don and stood looking down at him. "Let's keep this in-house shall we. No washing dirty linen and all that." It suddenly hit him. He leaned over and put his hand on the back of the chair towering over Don's seated figure. "For fuck's sake you've already told him." His voice became louder and filled with anger. "You little shit."

"Hear me out will you. At least do that before jumping to conclusions." Don heaved himself up from the chair and brushing past Andy, turned to face him.

"I've known Vincent for years. You know I nearly joined Floyds Chemist before deciding to come and work for you. I happened to bump into Vincent and we had a drink. He told me that he was looking for a good return on some money he had in his pension fund. Asked me if I had any ideas."

"So what's this got to do with me?" Andy resumed pacing around the office.

"I thought if he lent you the money at a good rate of interest it would get you off the hook. With the Swedish deal you could take a hefty dividend and pay him back."

Andy stopped and slumped down behind his desk. "And what's in it for you? I suppose you want a cut do you?" He sneered.

"As Finance Director I'm supposed to control the finances. I haven't been doing that. If word got out I could kiss goodbye to any of the non-exec jobs I've been put up for."

"Are you sure that's all, to protect your good name?" Andy folded his arms. "What time are we meeting?"

Typical thought Don. Bloody arrogance just because it's me he's meeting he hasn't got a clue. "10.00 o'clock here in your office."

"Let me think about it overnight. I'll give you my answer first thing. By the way, how much is he thinking of, have you any idea?"

Don managed to suppress the elation he felt as he stood up. You're on the hook you bugger. Walking toward the door he turned. "He talked about half a million pounds."

***

Since their meeting on Monday evening Vincent had spent most of Tuesday morning with his solicitor outlining the terms of the loan. Wednesday afternoon had also been spent with the solicitor this time reading through the draft and making minor changes.

"I'll collect the final version in the morning, say 9.30. Two copies but I want them loose bound. You know holes punched through and that fancy red ribbon you lawyers like threaded through to hold it all together."

He was on his way home when his mobile rang. "Floyd." His telephone voice was deep and stern.

"Vincent it's me, Don." Vincent could hear the excitement in his voice even at the end of a telephone. "I think we're on. He almost wet himself when I mentioned half a million. Is everything OK your end?"

"I'm collecting copies of the agreement in the morning. They'll be loose bound so we can take out the page with the default clause. He won't know what's hit him. When do you want me there?"

"He wants to think about it overnight. I told him you knew nothing about his taking money from the company but that you had a pension fund nest egg you needed to invest. I'm sure he'll want to meet. We'll just have to persuade you to part with your money." They both laughed.

"I'll give you a call soon after 9.00 when I've spoken to him." Don rang off.

Andy was on a high. Everything was coming together. He was annoyed that he had allowed Don to catch him out but in a roundabout way it proved to be the answer he was looking for. He sat back in his chair. Yes if he could get his hands on that sort of money to fund his sure fire bet he'd be in the clear.

"God but I feel randy." He said to no one. He pulled back his cuff and looked at his watch six thirty - a bit too late to call Miriam, Vincent might be at home, so who else was there that could satisfy the lust he felt.

"I'm going now Andy." Debbie put her head round the door. "I've almost finished the typing the notes on the Swedish deal I'll have them on your desk first thing. Is there anything else you need before I go?"

Andy looked up. "Come in Debbie. Shut the door behind you."

At five foot eight inches tall and a size ten with ash blond hair Debbie was attractive rather than pretty. All Andy could see though was the cleavage that showed above the 'V' neck of her sweater filled by a pair of ample breasts. She came into the room.

He got up and pointed toward the sofa. "Come and sit down. It's about time that you and I had a little chat. How about a drink?"

"Gin and tonic please." Debbie sat down on the sofa and crossed her legs allowing her skirt to ride up. Andy let his eyes roam over the sheen of her tights before turning to a drinks cabinet in the corner of his office.

"You know what happened last time we had a little chat." Debbie smiled to herself at the thought. She fancied Andy like mad. He was a generous boss and she rather liked it when he paid her some attention. And well, he was rather good when it came to satisfying a girl.

"I enjoyed it, didn't you?" Andy spoke over his shoulder as he dropped ice into two glasses. Adding a hefty splash of gin he picked up the glasses and brought them over to the sofa. "Here hold these while I get some tonic from the fridge." He looked down at her legs.

Opening the tonic Andy poured some into each glass and putting the bottle onto the coffee table sat down next to Debbie. Turning toward her he put his arm along the back of the sofa his hand just resting on her shoulder.

"I just feel in need of a little female company right now." Taking a glass from her hand he raised it. "Cheers." They both sipped at their drinks.

Andy put his glass down on the table. "You haven't got to rush off home have you?" He dropped his hand lightly onto her leg and leaning forward kissed her neck.

"Since you put it like that, no I don't suppose I have." Debbie placed her glass beside Andy's as he moved his hand further up her leg. "Shall I lock the door or will you?" She breathed into his ear.

It was 7.30 when Andy climbed into his car for the drive home. Debbie had given him great sex and what with tension of the day and a gin and tonic he felt tired. "Home." He commanded his car phone.

"26245, hello." Suzanne's voice broke into his reminiscence of Debbie's performance as she answered the phone.

"Hello darling, on my way from the office. How about a nice piece of steak and a bottle of red wine?"

"That sounds good. I've a few new potatoes and some salad. We could have cheese after."

"I'll be about half an hour see you then." He rang off and concentrated on keeping the car moving at a steady pace through the evening traffic.

Suzanne hummed to herself as she got two fillet steaks from the freezer and put them into the microwave to defrost. It wasn't often that Andy rang like that, she thought, he must be in a good mood.

She put the potatoes on to steam. Adding a large sprig of mint and a sprinkling of salt she put the lid on and turned up the gas. Her mind wandered. She imagined him standing behind her arms round her waist whispering in her ear. He was undoing the buttons of her blouse. The pinging of the microwave broke into her daydream. She switched on the oven and set the temperature to 100° centigrade ready to warm two plates.

On an impulse she ran up the stairs and into the bedroom. Taking off the skirt and blouse that she'd been wearing she rifled through her wardrobe. A silk skirt with a matching camisole top caught her eye.

She opened a drawer and chose from it a black bra and a pair of lace trimmed black panties. Slipping out of her underwear, she rushed to the bathroom and had a hurried shower. When she had dried herself she picked up her bottle of Chanel No 5 eau de parfume and sprayed herself liberally. She wanted to be dressed and downstairs before Andy got home. Quickly she put on the black underwear and dressed in the silk skirt and top.

    Sitting at her dressing table she ran the comb through her hair. After glossing her lips with a carmine red satin sheen lipstick she added a quick touch of mascara to her eyelashes. She stood up. There Andy Clewer, she thought, refuse me if you can.

    The water in the steamer was dangerously low and boiling furiously by the time she got back downstairs to the kitchen. She lowered the gas and took out a cast iron griddle. Taking a packet of butter from the fridge she cut off a large piece and dropped it into the pan. She needed a bottle of brandy as she had decided to flambé the steaks. There was something sensual about the dowsing of the meat with alcohol, setting it on fire and swirling the flames round the pan. Besides which the taste was heavenly.

    She busied laying the table in the dining room. She used the fine bone china, crystal wine glasses and silver cutlery. Having put two candles on the table she stood back, admiring the room. The polished yew table gleamed in the light from the table lamps she had lit. All set for a romantic evening. She took a bottle of brandy from the drinks cabinet and went back to the kitchen. Opening a cupboard she selected a small glass bowl and put it on the worktop. She pulled a half-full bag of mixed salad leaves from the fridge and tipped them into the bowl.

    Putting two plates to warm she lit the gas under the griddle pan and turned on the oven. She took the steaks from the microwave and patted them dry with paper towels.

    She heard Andy's car crunch onto the drive before the headlights swept across the room as he turned toward the garage. She almost felt herself blush as she remembered her daydream. Perhaps he would come up behind her.

    "I'm in the kitchen darling." She called as she heard the front door open. "You've got time for a quick wash before supper."

    "I think I'll have a shower." He was eager to get rid of any traces of Debbie before his wife got too close to him. "I won't be long. Pour me a drink there's an angel." He went up the stairs two at a time.

Suzanne poured two glasses of sauvignon blanc. The potatoes had finished cooking a while ago and she put them into a dish and into the warm oven. The butter in the pan was foaming so she turned the heat down to its lowest setting. Sprinkling the steaks with sea salt she added two twists of ground black pepper to each.

She could hear Andy moving about the bedroom as he got ready to come down.

"Glass of white wine for you, shall I bring it up?" She called picking up the two glasses in readiness to climb the stairs.

"I'll only be two ticks just putting my shirt on." He answered as he fastened the buttons on his shirt.

Moments later Andy walked into the kitchen. Taking a glass from her hand he gave Suzanne a peck on the cheek. "Thanks darling, cheers."

She raised her glass in salute and they both took mouthful of the chilled wine. Andy pulled a face. "Smells like cat's pee and tastes like gooseberries. Give me good old chardonnay any day. "He put his glass down. "I'll go and sort out a nice bottle of red to take the taste away."

He wandered off to the cupboard under the stairs that he called his wine cellar missing the look of disappointment on Suzanne's face at his rebuff. "There's a good Australian Cabernet-Shiraz that will suit down to the ground." She could just hear his muffled voice as she dropped the steaks onto the griddle and turned up the heat.

"Hurry up then the steaks are on the griddle. I've laid the table in the dining room so take the bottle through will you?"

"Dining room on a Wednesday and no guests. Have I missed something?" Andy pulled the cork on the bottle which came out with a satisfying thwack.

"I thought it would be nice, just the two of us, you know a bit of romance. Light the candles there's a dear."

Suzanne mixed walnut oil and Dijon mustard into a dressing. She spooned the dressing over the salad leaves. Taking the brandy, she poured a generous slug over the steaks on the hot griddle. There was a whoosh as the spirit ignited. She gulped back the last of her white wine.

She took the potatoes from the oven and put them onto the warm plates. The flames had died down so she switched off the gas and put a steak onto each plate, tipping the aromatic, buttery pan juices over them. Putting everything onto a tray she went through into the dining room.

Andy was already seated and halfway through a glass of the red. "There we are darling." She set a plate in front of him. "You haven't lit the candles."

"Bloody stupid idea, candles." He waved his glass. "We need a proper light on to see what we're doing."

Ignoring him Suzanne took a box of matches from the sideboard drawer and lit the candles. "There, that's more romantic." She blew out the match and sat down.

They completed the remainder of the meal in candlelight making small talk with Andy steadily emptying the bottle of red wine almost single handed.

"Come into the lounge and sit with me." She took hold of his hand and placed it gently on her breast. "I do want you Andy, please."

He lurched to his feet and looked at his wife's dumpy figure. He thought of Debbie and the way she had been nearly insatiable. Sitting on his lap and moaning in his ear until he laid her back down onto the sofa in his office and took her with a roughness that satisfied them both. He thought of Miriam and the things they did together. How her fingers caressed him to an exquisite hardness and how those slim legs wrapped around him in a passionate ecstasy pulling him deeper inside her.

"Sorry Suzanne not tonight." His voiced slurred. The effects of the large gin and tonic and too many glasses of wine. "I'm off to bed." He moved unsteadily towards the door.

"But darling," cried Suzanne, "I've made a special effort. I'll do whatever you want only please take me to bed."

Andy turned back to face her. He could see through the silk camisole a roll of deathly white flesh where her bra was too tight for her ample frame. "Not now Suzanne, some other time." He gave an involuntary shudder as he turned and fumbled his way through the door. "I'll sleep in the spare room."

She stood there hearing him bump his way up the stairs. All she could see was the look of contempt in his eyes as he rejected her. Tears brimmed in her eyes. Why did he always treat her like this? Well not always. There had been times, much earlier times when he had been the one begging for her to make love to him.

"Sod the washing up." Her voice sounded loud and harsh in the now stillness of the dining room. "May as well drown my sorrows." She opened the drinks cabinet and took out a balloon glass. There was the bottle of fine champagne cognac left over from a dinner party and she half-filled the glass before taking a gulp.

Switching out the lights she groped her way to the stairs and made her way up to the bedroom.

Andy's clothes lay in a jumble on the bed where he had thrown them in his haste to get into the shower. She grabbed them and went to throw them on the floor. As she did a waft of perfume floated off his shirt.

She stopped and sniffed. It wasn't the Hermes aftershave that he normally wore. It was definitely a woman's perfume. It hit her suddenly – Classique by Jean Paul Gautier. Definitely a young woman's perfume.

"You shit Andy. No wonder you didn't want me. You'd just had some bimbo." She said the words aloud and her voice faltered.

Jumping off the bed she marched across the landing and into the guest bedroom ready to fight it out with him. Andy was spark out on the bed, fully clothed with the bedside light on. A decanter and a tumbler with the dregs of the malt whisky in the bottom told its own story. He was drunk and out for the count.

Slamming the door behind her brought no more than an extra loud snort from the inert body on the bed. Running back to her own room Suzanne felt the tears sting in her eyes and overflow down her face.

She slumped down on the stool in front of the dressing table and grabbed at a box of tissues. In the mirror she could see a red-eyed runny nosed fat face looking back at her. Sniffing back more tears she snatched at her brandy glass.

"I'll get you for this Andy Clewer." She raised the glass. "That's a promise I'll keep, no matter how long it takes."

Chapter 14

Andy woke that Thursday morning with a splitting headache. The inside of his mouth tasted of last night's whiskey. At first he couldn't remember why he was in the guest bedroom and not in his own bed.

"Oh bugger." He mumbled to himself as the recollection of Suzanne's attempt to seduce him into bed hit him. As he sat up and swung his legs out of the bed he realised he was still fully clothed.

He glanced at the bedside table stifling a groan as he took in the half-empty whiskey decanter and tumbler. But it was the alarm clock that grabbed his attention – the digital display indicating that the time was 7.58 am.

"Bloody hell." Andy swore out loud and pushed himself off the bed as the recollection of the meeting with Don and Vincent Floyd later that day forced its way into his drink-fuddled brain. Marching out of the room and across the landing he stormed into their bedroom. It was empty. The bed had been made and the curtains were wide open.

Thrusting all thoughts of Suzanne from his mind he concentrated on getting out of his crumpled clothes and into the bathroom. The steaming shower began to revive him and his thoughts began to run more coherently toward the meeting. The strategy Don had outlined was good. He started to feel better.

He shaved and hurriedly dressed, steeling himself for the inevitable showdown with Suzanne. But the thought of getting his hands on the money that Don had talked about made him smile as he went down the stairs.

"Morning darling." He shoved open the kitchen door. "Sorry about last night I've got a lot on my mind at work and I." He looked round the empty kitchen.

"Suzanne." He raised his voice. "Suzanne where are you? I've said I'm sorry, are you there?"

It was then that he saw the post-it-note stuck to the front of the microwave. Pacing across the kitchen he snatched at the note.

Scanning it he read – 'Gone out today might be back later. Suzanne.' Oh sod the silly bitch. She'll be back alright,' Andy mused as he crumpled up the note and chucked it toward the rubbish bin.

He boiled the kettle and made himself a cup of instant coffee as he calculated how to play the meeting that morning. He checked the time – 8.30 – yes Don should be at his desk by now.

Picking up his coffee he made his way into the study. Sitting at the desk he pulled the telephone toward him and dialled Don's direct line.

"Don Markham." The phone had hardly rung and it was as if Don was eager to answer in the hope it was Andy.

"Don, Andy here – our meeting this morning." He paused. "Let's just say I am prepared to meet with Vincent and to hear what he has to say."

"You won't regret it Andy." And neither will I thought Don as he tried hard to keep his voice normal. "I'll give Vincent a call and set things up. Get him in about 10.30 like we said yesterday?"

"That's fine. See you later." Andy rang off and sipped at his coffee turning over in his mind how he would transfer that amount of cash to Miriam in time for her to place the bet.

He left the empty cup on the desk as he went in search of his car keys. Three minutes later he was slamming the front door and climbing into the car for the journey to the office.

"Morning Debbie and how's my favourite secretary this morning?" Andy winked at her as he breezed into the office. Leaning forward he gave her a quick kiss full on the lips.

She jumped up from her work station and moved toward him. Checking that the door was closed she pressed herself against him. "You did better than that yesterday." She breathed into his ear and pulling his head down she kissed him with an open mouth and exploring tongue.

He pulled back from her. "Steady I've got an important meeting today and I need all my strength." His mouth twitched up at the corner in a wicked smile. "Now after the meeting that might be different."

Pulling a tissue from her pocket Debbie carefully wiped traces of lipstick from Andy's mouth. "Yes boss." She giggled. "I'll be ready to take down dictation or anything else you might want."

Laughing Andy strode through into his own office. "Tell Don I'm in will you." He called over his shoulder. "And get me some coffee and a pastry or a biscuit or something."

About ten minutes later Don followed Debbie into Andy's office. "I've put extra cups and got some shortbread," she said as she set a tray down on the meeting table that extended at right angles from Andy's desk. She poured two cups and handed one to each of them. "Give me a shout if you need anything else."

"Vincent Floyd will be joining us." Don said as Debbie reached the door. "Just show him in when he arrives."

She glanced toward Andy who moved his head slightly in confirmation. She smiled and nodded at Don as she turned and closed the door.

The two men sat down. Andy gravitating naturally to the head of the table with Don taking a seat on his right.

"So how will the deal work?" He shot a puzzled look at Don. "And what does Vincent Floyd get out of this?"

"I think it's better if we wait for him to explain matters. He just thinks he could help you and improve his pension fund at the same time. Let's face it, he knows how successful your business is if you just look at the turnover he's doing on our products."

With Vincent arriving in less than half-an-hour Andy missed the emphasis made on the 'your business' his mind too busy looking for angles on the proposed deal.

It seemed appropriate that they were going through the last quarter's sales figures that showed turnover up by 15% year on year when Debbie knocked on the door and ushered Vincent Floyd into the room.

"Tea or coffee, Mr Floyd?" Debbie smiled as she moved over to the meeting table. "Would you like a shortbread as well?"

"Just coffee's fine thanks." Vincent strode confidently toward the meeting table, hand outstretched. "Andy, good of you to see me." He put his slim leather briefcase onto a chair.

Andy stood up and the two shook hands. "Don." Vincent waved in Don's direction.

The three men sat down. Debbie placed a cup of coffee in front of Vincent and left the room. Don looked expectantly at Vincent who was about to speak when Andy cut him off.

"Well, Don." He said a frown creasing his brow. "Perhaps you'd better explain what this meeting is all about."

Don hadn't expected this and he wasn't prepared to take the lead. He turned hesitantly toward Vincent. "We were talking the other night – having a drink for old time's sake – and Vincent was telling me how he needed some advice on making an investment for his pension fund."

Vincent nodded. By the less than confident tone of his voice he could sense that Don was on a wing and a prayer. If nothing else Andy Clewer was a smart operator and one wrong word could upset his plans to get even.

"That's right." Vincent gave a small laugh. "Don said that you might be able to help. Look, I won't beat about the bush. I've got half a million pounds that I need to invest – discreetly – if you know what I mean."

"I see, all well and good for you so what's in it for me? Andy looked at first one and then the other.

"You get the use of my money for an agreed period of time and when you give it back you add a bonus of ten percent. Of course I'd need some form of collateral, not that I don't trust you but half a million is a lot of money."

Standing up Andy moved round toward the window. The light streaming through silhouetted his figure and made the others screw up their eyes in an attempt to see him. He felt good. He had them at a disadvantage. Don was up to something he was sure but he couldn't figure out whether Vincent Floyd was being used or not.

"How long do I get to use this money of yours?" He moved his position so that Vincent had to turn in his seat to keep looking at him. He was enjoying this.

"I had in mind six months. That takes you to the end of your financial year. How does that sound?"

"The timing sounds good but I don't like the ten percent - I would've thought that five would have been ample." Andy paused and inclined his head savouring the control he felt over the meeting. "Given that you wanted to be discreet."

Vincent stood up. "Seven and a half percent and we've got a deal. I'm sure that half a million pounds will come in handy. Don told me you were expanding in Scandinavia so you might need to buy more plant to increase production."

The strident chirping of Andy's phone cut through the tension that had built up between the three men. Andy relinquished his position in the window, snatched up the handset and barked at the voice on the other end. "Bloody hell, Debbie I don't want any interruptions. Who is it anyway?"

"It's the bank wanting to arrange a meeting with you. They wouldn't take no for an answer. What shall I tell them?

Don and Vincent couldn't hear what Debbie told him but they could see his face change as the colour drained from it. "Make it." He quickly worked out in his mind. The race was in less than ten days. The money from the bet would be into Miriam's account almost immediately. All he had to do was get it transferred into his own account to clear his overdraft. "Make in two weeks' time. Either here or at their place I don't mind."

He jammed the receiver down. With a couple of swift strides he moved round the table to stand in front of Vincent. "Shake on it." He blew out his cheeks in a sigh. "Providing we can agree on the collateral."

"Vincent stood and held out his hand. "I can't see that being a problem – after all it's only a formality amongst friends." Andy gripped his hand and the two men smiled at each other.

Vincent moved to pick up his briefcase. "I took the liberty of having my solicitors draw up an outline agreement that should serve the purpose. There are blank spaces for the interest and length of time the," he coughed to cover the near slip of calling it a loan, "the investment remains with you."

He saw Andy's face change from a smile to a scowl. "Taking me for granted were you?"

Unperturbed Vincent continued. "And also I took the liberty." He reached into the briefcase and pulled out a piece of paper. "Of having this Bankers Draft prepared in the sum of half a million. Negotiable through any bank." He leaned forward and placed it in front of Andy.

No matter how hard he tried Andy couldn't help but look down. There it was. The way out of all his problems. He managed to keep his face expressionless.

"So what about this collateral?" He didn't realise it but he had picked up the bankers draft and was holding it in both hands.

Vincent gave a self-satisfied smile. Greed had won the day for him. "Oh, I don't know – what's your place at Crondall worth?"

Andy shook his head. "The bank has already beaten you to that I'm afraid. There's the horses."

"Technically they belong to the company." Don spoke for the first time since he opened the meeting.

"Well there's my shares in the business." Andy shrugged his shoulders. "But they're worth far more than half a million pounds."

"It's only to keep the trustees of the fund happy. As I said we're amongst friends so your shares would be safe. So what do you think?" Vincent kept his voice light and he spread his hands out toward Andy, palms uppermost.

Andy was hardly listening. His mind was already working on how to get the money into Miriam's account with Leisure Industries. His eyes fixed on the row of noughts on the bankers draft.

Vincent glanced across to Don and raised his eyebrows. "Andy – I said what do you think?"

Andy nodded as he tore his eyes away from the draft. "Ok, you've got yourself a deal. I'll just put this away." He opened his desk drawer and placed the draft carefully on top of his desk diary. "What do we need to do now?"

Vincent pulled two copies of the agreement from his case. Before arriving he had undone the ribbon that had held the pages together and had used paper clips instead.

"We need to fill in the blank spaces. You and I need to sign and we can get Don to be our witness. Keep everything between us." He gave a small laugh. "And the solicitors of course – but they don't count.

Don, you're the finance man. Can you fill in the blanks for us?" He pushed the papers over to Don.

Andy gazed out of the window thinking about Miriam. "I've got a lunch appointment can you hurry things up Don?"

"Almost finished. If you just sign here and here." He pointed with his pen before passing it to Andy.

Andy reached into his inside pocket. "I'll use the gold Mont Blanc if you don't mind. More in keeping with the deal."

In pretence of reading the agreement Andy turned the pages. They weren't numbered but he didn't notice. He noted the sum of money involved and the rate of interest but didn't pay much attention to anything else. With a flourish he signed where Don had indicated.

"Don't worry if you want to get off for your appointment." Vincent put his hand on Andy's shoulder. "Don and I can get the rest of this sorted out. I'll sign and we'll get the copies bound up. I will need to lodge evidence of your holding in the company."

Andy stood up and folded the Banker's Draft into his inside pocket. "Don's got my share certificate in the safe. Vincent, you're a good friend." He held out his hand. "I must dash."

"Have a good lunch and take care of that piece of paper." Vincent shook his hand and watched as Andy paced with indecent haste from the room.

I'm going out now Debbie. I'll be out of contact and I won't be back today." He waved over his shoulder as he marched down the corridor.

Vincent turned toward Don. "I think we'll number the pages now Don. Once we've added this one with a default date that calls for the sum to be repaid on demand."

"Can I use my biro or should I go out and get a gold Mont Blanc?" The two men started to laugh.

Debbie put her head through the door. "Everything OK or is there anything else I can get for you?" She smiled but there was no light in her eyes. Andy had completely forgotten their kiss earlier that morning.

Don struggled to bring his laughter under control. "Everything's fine Debbie – just fine. Close the door there's a good girl."

Chapter 15

Stuffing his mobile phone into his pocket Andy left the office in a hurry. Once out of the door he ran toward his car. He was elated and as soon as he sat down behind the wheel he scrabbled in his pocket for the phone.

Punching in a number he gabbled with excitement when Miriam answered. "It's in my pocket, the money, I've got it. We need to put it into your bank and get the big bet set up."

"Whoa, slow down." Miriam almost reeled from the breathless onslaught. "Where are you?"

"I'm just leaving the office and getting into my car. Tell me where your bank is and I'll meet you there."

"Not so fast, you can buy me a decent lunch and when we've finished, then we'll go to the bank."

"Ok, Ok. But where?" He started the car and pulled out of his parking space and headed for the exit to the car park.

Debbie watched him from her office window. She saw how excited he was. He had never even given her a second glance as he hurried out of the office. She felt the disappointment like a ton weight on her shoulders. She had convinced herself that she was more to him than just a quick tumble. Slowly the realisation dawned on her. She was just being used to satisfy him when there was no one else.

Laughter came from behind the closed door to Andy's office. She listened. Those two were up to something. Usually she would have told him but, well serves him right. She picked up her bag and set off for the canteen. Let them get on with it she thought bitterly.

Miriam was to meet Andy at Bentalls department store in Kingston. There was an Italian restaurant on the first floor that served light lunches. It was a busy place that hummed with the sound of happy chatter. There were friends meeting and swapping news and shoppers showing off their newly purchased bargains and comparing prices. It was the ideal place to meet and not be noticed.

Just for one fleeting moment, as he drove out of the car park, the thought that he should use the money to pay off his debts slipped into his mind. Putting his foot hard down on the accelerator he sped down the road, all thoughts of paying off his debts driven from his mind. The only thought that stayed with him was that he was within reach of pulling off the biggest winning bet of his life.

They had arranged to meet at midday and Andy was already there when Miriam walked in.

"You're late. Where have you been?" He didn't even stand up or give her a kiss. He grabbed her hand and pulled her down onto the seat beside him. "How far to the bank?"

"Can we have lunch first? She wrested her hand free. "I'm starving. The bank is just over the road in Church Street, two minutes away." She settled back in her seat. "It's no use going now all the office people will be queuing in their lunch hour, let's leave it a half hour or so."

Andy could see the sense in what she was saying and reluctantly agreed to lunch first.

A young waitress appeared beside their table. "Hi I'm Angie and I will be looking after you today. The special is aubergine parmigiana and it comes with a mixed salad."

"That'll do just fine for us both and two large glasses of house red" Andy paused, and some garlic bread while we wait."

"No problem and I'll bring you some tap water." Angie smiled at them both and moved off toward the kitchens.

She pulled a face. "I'd rather have white but of course the master has to take over and I don't get a look in."

"If you don't want it I'll bloody well drink it." Andy snapped glaring at her and leaning forward. "I didn't realise you were that fussy when someone else was buying."

"Here we are, garlic bread and two large glasses of red, it's Chianti if that's OK?" Angie placed a plate in front of each of them together with glasses of red wine before putting the dish of garlic bread in the centre of the table.

Andy nodded to the waitress as Miriam shrugged her shoulders and picked up her glass. He put his hand on her wrist, stopping her from raising the glass to her lips.

"Just a second." He picked up his glass and lifted it toward her. "Here's to the big win." They touched glasses. "Cheers."

She responded in a dull voice feeling once again that he took her for granted.

They sat in silence until Angie reappeared bearing two plates of steaming aubergine parmigiana. "Here we are, knives and forks, serviettes." She placed everything down on the table. "Enjoy."

Of course Andy didn't notice a thing. He just had to show Miriam the Banker's draft. "There it is." He whisked the draft from his inside pocket a huge grin across his face. "You pay that in and we'll take- oh I don't know – say ten thousand pounds and get a trip sorted out right away. How does that sound?"

Andy's excitement was infectious and the thought of having ten thousand pounds to spend on a trip very much appealed to Miriam and her mood changed. "It sounds marvellous." She leaned over and kissed him. "What about one of those Pacific Islands? Can we fly first class this time? I've always fancied myself swanning through the gate with some little man carrying our luggage running along behind."

"And we need to get a bet on as soon as we can." He hadn't heard a word she'd said, his mind working overtime on the thought of the vast amount of money he would be getting in a few days' time.

But first they had to get to the bank. As they ate he would glance every couple of minutes at his watch. The hands seemed to crawl round the dial. He fidgeted in his seat, unable to sit still for more than a couple of moments, the draft practically burning a hole in his pocket. Every now and then his hand slid inside his jacket feeling into the pocket, touching the paper just to make sure it was still there.

They finished their meal and ordered coffee, neither of them wanting a dessert in spite of Angie trying to tempt them to tiramisu.

The moment the hands on his watch pointed at 12.45 Andy jumped up. "Come on Miriam, time to go." He was already turning away from the table.

"I'll just finish my coffee." Miriam moved to pick up her cup when Andy's hand clamped over her wrist.

"We've waited long enough." He leaned over her and hissed in her ear. "I want to get the money paid in and then get a bet sorted out – do you hear me?"

Miriam tried to pull her arm away. Andy put his other hand under her elbow and nearly lifted her off the seat as he levered her upwards.

"Alright, alright I'm getting up." Her voiced grew louder as he exerted more pressure. "You're hurting me." She shrieked. People at the nearby tables stopped eating and turned to watch.

"I'm sorry darling; I was trying to help you." Andy realised that they were becoming the centre of attention, the last thing he wanted. He let go of Miriam's wrist, whisked her jacket off the back of the chair and held it out for her. "Come on, it's time we were off."

Standing up Miriam slipped into her coat. "You act like an ape-man sometimes." She mumbled rubbing gingerly at the shape of Andy's fingers imprinted on her wrist. Not for the first time she wondered if she should make the break from him.

Ignoring her, Andy led the way out of the restaurant and headed toward the escalator. Turning to make sure that Miriam was following he stepped onto the moving staircase and they descended to the ground floor.

"Which way now?" Seemingly with a mind of its own, his hand slipped once again into his inside jacket pocket.

"Over there on the corner of Church Street."

Tucking her arm through his Miriam was dragged along as Andy pounded across the road and headed toward the bank.

Inside the bank she turned to him. "Do I just walk up to the counter and pay it in like a normal cheque? I mean it is rather a large amount of money."

This was not something he'd thought about and she was right. You couldn't march up to the counter and stick half a million pounds into your account.

Glancing round Andy saw an information desk. He strode over and addressed the girl sitting there looking in a bored fashion at a screen on the desk. "Good afternoon. We have a rather large transaction to carry out and we would like some help and..." He gazed round the crowded banking hall. "Some privacy."

The girl looked up. "Have you got an appointment?" She smiled. "Our personal bankers don't see anyone without an appointment, I'm sorry."

Leaning on the desk Andy towered over her. "You will be sorry. We need to move half a million pounds around and I'm sure that one of the bankers will make an exception if you tell them the size of the transaction." His voice carried menace as he spoke quietly between gritted teeth. He smiled and patted her hand. "Now why don't you pick up that phone and get someone down to see us. There's a good girl."

He straightened up and watched as the girl lifted the receiver and punched three digits. A voice answered. "I've got mister." She hesitated and nervously looked up at Andy. "What was the name sir?"

Andy pointed at Miriam. "It's Mrs Floyd."

"A Mrs Floyd who would like to speak to a personal banker, in private, about a large deposit." The voice the other end clattered in the earpiece. "No, no appointment but they say..." She paused. "It's half a million pounds."

Putting down the receiver she said to Andy. "Mr Brevin, our deputy manager will be down right away. If you would like to take a seat." She pointed to a row of chairs.

"We'll wait here thank you." Andy's hand moved to his inside jacket pocket – he felt the piece of paper. Yes it was still there.

Within a few minutes they were greeted by a tall, thin balding man. "Mrs Floyd, Ron Brevin, Deputy Manager." He held out his hand and nodded at Andy. "If you come with me there's a small interview room we can use."

With the door closed Andy took over. "Mrs Floyd has sold her share in a hotel venture." He explained. "She has this Banker's draft she needs to deposit." He pulled it from his pocket. "And wants it kept safe before completing another deal. She'll be drawing on it over the next few days." He paused. "But wants some of the cash now."

He received a nasty jolt when the deputy manager accepted the story with a nod. "I recognised you right away, Mr Clewer. Normally there would be a number of formalities to go through. Money laundering and so on. However, with someone as well-known as you, I don't believe I need to bother you with of all that." He raised his eyebrows. "However, even a bankers draft takes a few days to clear but I think it would be in order to allow an advance." He turned to Miriam. "How much are you wanting Mrs Floyd?"

Glancing at Andy she said. "Ten thousand pounds."

He used the phone on the table to authorise the payment. "They'll bring the money down in an envelope. Is there anything else I can do for you Mrs Floyd?"

Miriam shook her head. "I don't think so." They made small talk for a few minutes before there was a knock on the door.

"Ah here's the cash now." Mr Bevin stood up and opening the door took an envelope from the young woman who stood there. "I just need you to sign this." He put down a completed withdrawal slip. "And you need this receipt to show you've paid in half a million pounds." With some difficulty Miriam managed to tuck the envelope into her handbag.

Moments later they were escorted to the door of the bank. Having shaken hands with Mr Brevin Andy couldn't wait to get outside.

"Look, over there." He pointed to a small doorway almost opposite the bank on the other side of the road. "That's an internet café. We can get our first bet on."

As he hurried Miriam across the she tried to speak to him. "But I...." "You can tell me later." Andy snapped.

He barged his way through the midst of a crocodile of school children, oblivious to the shouts from their teacher. He relentlessly guided her toward the café cursing at an old man with a Zimmer frame who couldn't get out of his way and was brushed sideways with a sweep of an arm. He felt his excitement growing with every stride. The sooner the bets were placed the sooner he could relax and look forward to his winnings.

Barging through the doorway he marched up to the counter. "Give me a 10 minute slot." He told the spotty youth pulling the handle on an espresso machine. "And hurry up will you."

"Nothing free for the next hour, mate" said the youth turning his head to look over his shoulder.

Andy became aware of Miriam tugging at his arm. "It's no use Andy, I haven't got the password or account number with me." She gave a small smile. "Sorry."

116

"Shall I book you slot or what?" asked the youth as he stood leaning on the counter facing them.

"Fuck off." Andy was livid. The money was there and he couldn't get his bet on. Turning away from the counter he grabbed Miriam by the arm and roughly pulled her out into the street.

"You stupid bitch. What's the point in getting the money and not being able to place a bet? No bloody brains. Oh yes you know what to do in bed alright - bright enough for that. Well you had better get off home and get it sorted." He paused. "No wait. I'll take you home and we can put the bet on from your place."

He hustled Miriam back to Bentalls. He had left his car in their car park. Within minutes they were speeding down the exit ramp and out onto the one way system. Miriam sat beside him not saying a word. Her arm was hurting where Andy had grabbed her and almost dragged her to the car park. Dark thoughts raced through her mind. She was being used and she decided that she didn't like it one bit. But she was afraid of him and his temper.

Chapter 16

It was nearly 1.00pm when Suzanne let herself into the house knowing that Andy would be well out of the way at this time of the day. All morning she had wandered aimlessly around the shops. In her mind seeing images of Andy in bed with some girl. She couldn't stop imagining what they might do to each other. How he might touch and caress her – how she might touch him.

It was all too much. She shuddered. Perhaps a drink would help. Make her forget. Numb her mind and wipe out the images of Andy naked on top of a slim body. She glanced at herself in the hall mirror. Dumpy, red-eyed and with hair, normally groomed to perfection, looking like a brillo pad. Tears welled up and ran down her cheeks.

Quickly turning away from the sad woman in the mirror she almost ran into the lounge and clutched at a tumbler on the top of the drinks cabinet. She grabbed a bottle and poured. Her hand was shaking as she lifted the glass to her mouth and took a swallow. It was whisky, although to her there was no taste. Just a burning sensation as the liquid made its way down her throat.

She walked toward the kitchen carrying the bottle in one hand, the tumbler in the other. Glancing into the study as she passed she could see that Andy had left an empty coffee cup on the desk and she looked at it with disgust.

"That's all I'm good for." She spoke out loud. "To clear up after you, you filthy bastard."

The phone rang making her jump. Whisky splashed onto her skirt. "Bugger, bugger, bugger!" She grabbed the phone. "Yes".

"Suzanne, it's me - Vincent Floyd." A strident voice sounded in her ear. "I must see you. You and I have got to talk. There's something….."

"Vincent." She interrupted him, choking back a sob. "Look, I'm not being rude but I really don't feel like seeing or talking to anybody at the moment."

"Are you alright?" She could hear that there was a puzzled concern in his voice and it heightened her emotions that someone felt concern for her.

"Yes – I'm fine". She couldn't help it. The tears flowed down her cheeks. Sniffing she tried to stop them. Since the night before all she'd thought about was Andy with some woman. His hands caressing her. Her arms holding him. "No," she sobbed, "I'm not; fine that is."

"Suzanne, I'm coming right over and I'm not taking no for an answer." Before she could respond he hung up.

Looking at the bottle she thought about having another drink. Perhaps not if Vincent really was coming over. Picking up the bottle she walked slowly to the drawing room and put it away in the cabinet. Could she face Vincent – should she tell him? It might be better if she did. Sitting down, her mind immediately returned to thoughts of Andy. Unfaithful, treacherous Andy in bed – his tongue exploring....

"Stop it." She jumped up. "I must get on and do something, not just sit here."

Wandering out into the hall she saw the mirror and remembered what a mess she looked. Running upstairs she pulled off her clothes and dived into the shower. Fifteen minutes later, sitting in front of her dressing table she finished drying her hair. Unplugging the hairdryer she put it back into the drawer. She smoothed a light foundation onto her face and adding a touch of lipstick she began to feel better.

She heard a car crunch up to the front of the house and stop. Nervously she peered out from behind the curtains. No it wasn't Andy – it was Vincent Floyd.

She rushed down the stairs almost stumbling in her haste to open the front door and watched as Vincent climbed out of his car and strode toward her.

"Suzanne." Vincent took her hand and they moved into the hall. Pulling away from him she turned and closed the door.

"Oh Vincent, I'm so sorry…" Choking back her tears she struggled to stop herself from breaking down. "It's just." She paused. "Andy's having an affair." There she said it.

"Oh Suzanne, my poor dear." He put his arm round her shoulders and led her through to the kitchen and spotting the glass with the remains of the whisky Suzanne had left on the draining board he tipped the contents down the sink. "Let's have a cup of tea; we really do need to talk."

Pleased to be able to do something Suzanne moved to the sink. Picking up the kettle she ran cold water until it was half-full. "There are cups and saucers in the cupboard behind you." She plugged in the kettle, switched it on and searched on the shelf above the worktop. "Earl Grey, is that OK?"

"Fine by me." Vincent's voice was muffled as he reached into the tall cupboard for the cups and saucers.

With their tea made they sat at the kitchen table. "He phoned me from the car, said he was on his way home. He doesn't do that very often. I thought we could have a romantic evening." She blew her nose.

"You don't have to tell me you know." Vincent smiled sympathetically. "But if it helps."

Suzanne carried on as if she hadn't heard him. "I'd gone to a lot of trouble. Nice meal, candles on the table, I'd even put on sexy underwear in the hope that maybe he might - you know. But what did he do? Got rat-arsed that's what." She stood up and moved restlessly around the table. "He'd been with another woman before he came home I smelt the perfume on the shirt he had been wearing that he had just dumped on the bed."

Vincent took a deep breath and steeled himself for had to tell her before she carried on any more. "Look, there's no other way of saying this but he's having an affair with Miriam." He blurted it out.

"With Miriam." She looked at him in amazement. "But how, when?" She stumbled over her words. "I don't understand."

"They went to the races together." His face twisted into a sour grin. "A golfing pal of mine said he saw them. I borrowed a video of the race. It was them alright. Smiling and cuddling close together as they got some prize or the other – and they've been away together."

"Well maybe racing was just a bit of..." She paused. "Innocent fun. I don't always like going to the races. As for going away, Andy hasn't been away anywhere as far as I can recall."

"Do you remember that night you rang for Miriam? I'd just come back from Switzerland. I think I must have sounded surprised to hear you asking for her."

"Yes I remember. You didn't recognise my voice but why do you think they've been away somewhere?"

"They were away then. Somewhere hot because she had a suntan although she came out with some story about being under someone's sun lamp."

"But Andy wasn't away with Miriam he was visiting a client's stores in East Anglia. Oh my God." Suzanne's hand flew to her mouth. "He said he was visiting your stores with you."

"Almost perfect. You think he was with me and Miriam told me she was staying with you while I was in Switzerland well out of the way."

"Perfect that is until you and I talk which I guess they thought would never happen." Suzanne blew her nose.

"I need to know what you're going to do now you've found out. He's up to eyes in debt you know." Vincent patted her hand.

"The bastard. All that show, entertaining, horses and you say it's all borrowed money. At least the house is in my name so he can't get his grubby paws on that." She spat the words out.

"I don't know what he told you but the bank has lent him money secured against the house. You must have signed something agreeing to it."

Her puzzled frown turned to a look of hatred. "I trusted him. He says don't worry it's only a formality so I never really read the papers just signed. He never tells me anything, what he's doing, where he's going. He treats me like dirt."

She gave a thin smile. "Do you know you getting the cups and saucers out of the cupboard is more than he's done in the kitchen for months and months? That night when I thought we were going to make love he came home and just threw his clothes on the floor, had a shower and left them there. Expected me to pick them up." She laughed a nervous high pitched laugh. "That's when I smelt the perfume – Classique – and realised why he didn't want me. He just had. Oh Vincent I'm sorry. I didn't mean."

"What was that perfume again?" He cut in sharply.

"Classique, why?"

"Miriam only ever uses a perfume called Seduction. She's allergic to anything else. It makes her skin go dry and itchy."

"The sly little shit. Two timing me with Miriam and shagging some other bit on the side as well." The tears welled up in Suzanne's eyes and her voice thickened. She got up and gazed out of the window. "What a fool I've been. Played right into his hands – the doting little wife at home believing all those lies without question." She turned back quickly to face Vincent. "But what about you?" Her tone softened. "You've been hurt just as much as me."

"I love Miriam. I've thought long and hard about it but you know I can't ever think of being without her. Are you going to give him another chance?" Vincent spoke earnestly. "I have to know what you're going to do."

"I'd like to kick him in the balls and then out of my house." Venom oozed in her voice. "But you say the house isn't mine."

"I've got a plan but I need you with me." He glanced at his watch. "We've got a couple of hours are you with me?"

"If means getting rid of HIM." She couldn't bring herself to say Andy's name. "Then yes of course I am. But what about the house?"

"I can take care of the bank and make sure the house is yours again. You'll have to sign but this time you'll know what you're signing."

They moved through to the drawing room. "Would you like a drink?" Suzanne was determined to help Vincent if it meant getting her own back on Andy.

When she had poured them both a glass of wine Vincent outlined what he had in store for Andy. It was just after 4.30 when Suzanne saw him to the door.

"Remember my dear; you mustn't let on, just act normally." He gave her a peck on the cheek and started toward his car. He stopped and turned. "By the way did you know that all four of us are going to the races in a few days? I think that'll be fun don't you?"

She waved and watched as he climbed into his car. He started the engine and with a toot on the horn, sped down the drive and out of sight. She closed the door feeling more confident than she ever had done before. She couldn't help but laugh. In a few days Andy would be a broken man. This time she was in the know and revenge was going to be oh so sweet.

Chapter 17

Coming back from Kingston, Andy parked his car about quarter of a mile from the house in Richmond, just in case Vincent was at home. "Give me a call on the mobile if he's not in," he instructed Miriam. "If I don't hear from you by..." He pulled back his cuff and glanced at his watch. "Its 2.20 now – say by 2.30 I'll know he's in and I'll shoot off."

He grabbed her arm. "Whatever happens you must get the first bet placed. Listen carefully. If he's in then you'll have to put the bet on yourself. Bet five thousand pounds on Alternative Ways to lose the XYZ Handicap. Have you got that – to lose? She nodded. "You can ring me at the office in the morning and let me know. Don't let me down Miriam." He squeezed her arm with every word to emphasise his point. "I'm depending on you."

"But why back the horse to lose?" She frowned. "I don't understand surely you want it to win".

"Just bloody well go and do it. Leave the understanding to me." He leaned across her and pushed the door open. "Go on - we haven't got all bloody day."

She got out of the car tears, brimming in her eyes. She slammed the door shut and with her heels tapping on the pavement started to march down the road.

"Miriam." Andy's shout through the open driver's window stopped her in mid stride. "I think you'd better give me that envelope. If Vincent sees it he'll want to know where the money came from."

Retracing her steps she pulled the envelope from her bag, walked round the car and thrust into his face. "That's right; make sure you cover your tracks. Don't worry about me."

She turned abruptly and was moving away when Andy jumped out of the car. With a couple of swift paces he reached her. Putting both hands on her shoulders he pulled her to a halt. He gently turned her so as to face him.

"I'm sorry darling." His voice was low and seductive. "I really care about you and the thought of Vincent ruining our plans would be too much to bear. Forgive me?" He raised his eyebrows questioningly.

Miriam's mind was in turmoil. She gave him a half smile. "Of course I forgive you." Her head turned as she darted a glance up and down the road. "Look I must go. We don't want anyone seeing us standing here like this." She gave him a quick peck on the cheek and broke away from his grasp. "I'll ring you in the morning." She called over her shoulder fighting back the tears as once again she set off down the road.

There was no sign of Vincent as she let herself into the house. "Vincent." She called. "It's me. Are you home?" The silence of the house was reassuring as she stood there. Closing the front door she scurried into the kitchen. She called once more her voice trembling. "Vincent, are you there?"

Satisfied that she was alone she slumped down at the table. Putting her head into her hands she felt the tears welling up. Her shoulders shook as she sobbed. What a mess. One moment Andy was loving and thoughtful the next, a mean bully boy. How could she have been taken in by him? She felt trapped. The vicious streak that lay beneath the surface of his smooth ways and good looks frightened her.

Thinking back she began to catalogue all the humiliation, the pain and hurt he had caused her. The way he was obsessed with his gambling. How many bruises she had suffered - too many to count. The way he treated her in the restaurant at Kingston shouting and making a scene. There had been excitement that was true but all too often that had been overshadowed by his ability to hurt and humiliate her.

In her mind she listed the times he had taken her for granted, the times he had used her, the times he had physically hurt her. She tried to recall any occasion that he had just wanted to be with her as a person, for love and friendship and not just for sex. She looked for any little thing that might have balanced the book – nothing came to mind.

She thought of Vincent; a kind and gentle man who loved her deeply. A man who didn't need to show off, who was generous with his affection and was happy just to be with her. She didn't want to lose him. Her mind was made up – she would have nothing more to do with Andy. But how to walk away from him when he was so fired up about his big bet and had made it clear that he was depending on her. Her fingers explored her arm still tender from his tight grip. She realised that if things didn't go his way he would take it out on her.

She had no idea how long she sat there but it was dark when she heard a noise at the front door. She sat up trembling. "Oh my God it's Andy." Her hand flew to her mouth. How could she have forgotten all about him and the bet?

The front door opened and she heard footsteps in the hall and she recognised the pom-pom-pom of Vincent's attempt at singing. "I'm in here, Vincent." She called out as she dabbed at her face with a handkerchief, relief flooding through her body.

"What are doing sitting in here? Vincent switched on the lights as he walked into the kitchen. "You've got make-up all over your face – whatever's the matter? Come here." He held his arms open.

She jumped up and rushed to him. His arms closed round her and somehow she felt safe.

"You've been crying." He stood back and looked at her. "I think we should have a talk, don't you?"

"I don't know what you mean." Miriam's voice quavered. She sniffed and searched for her hanky to hide the anxiety that was building up inside.

Vincent bent down and picked up the handkerchief dropped when Miriam had jumped up. "Here, dry your eyes." He said kindly. "I think you do know. Let's talk about you and Andy Clewer."

Miriam felt her legs go weak and she had to grab hold of the back of the chair to stop herself from falling. The colour drained from her face. "You know?"

"Yes, I know. And so does Suzanne." She could hear the anger in his voice. "Here let's go and sit down where we can talk." He took her hand and led her into the lounge. "Sit here while I put some lights on."

Miriam sat wearily down on the sofa. "But how did you know? What's going to happen? Oh Vincent." Her voice broke and tears streamed down her face. "I'm so sorry it's just..."

"Shush. Don't say anymore just listen to me." Vincent sat down beside her and took her hand. "It doesn't matter how I know." He stopped, a look of pain on his face as he remembered watching the video of the two of them at the races. "It's what we're going to do that's important." His voice almost pleading. "Tell me it's over Miriam. Tell me he means nothing to you."

"I've been so stupid. It was such fun at first but he was just using me. I know that now. He's cruel, nasty and...." The words had been tumbling out and now she paused to take a deep breath. "Yes, Vincent, oh yes I want to leave him. I don't love him, I never have. It's just that he made things seem so exciting. The races, the Aston Martin, the Michelin starred restaurants. When I walked into anyplace with him they would bend over backwards to look after us. It was as if he had, I don't know a charisma, an aura.

She gazed into her husband's eyes. He just seemed to know how to get what he wanted." "You do believe me Vincent, don't you?

She looked so frail and vulnerable that Vincent had to take her in his arms. "Of course I believe you. I can see why you were taken in by his flash style." He smiled tenderly. "I know I'm a bit of an old fuddy-duddy. I don't drive an Aston Martin and I'd rather be tucked up in bed with a cup of cocoa than out clubbing or at some swanky restaurant. But I do love you and together we'll make sure that Andy Clewer doesn't come between us ever again. But I'll need your help, yours and Suzanne's."

"Oh my God, Suzanne." Miriam exclaimed. "You said she knew. I don't think I could ever face her."

"Yes you can. In fact we'll face her together. We need her to get that bastard stitched up so tight that he'll have trouble farting never mind breathing." Vincent laughed. "I've already started a little deception that will mean the end of Andy Clewer. Have you arranged to see him again?"

"No and I hope I never have to." She almost spat the words out. "But I'm supposed to ring him tomorrow to tell him about a bet."

"I didn't know that you knew anything about betting. What sort of a bet anyway?" Vincent sounded puzzled.

"He got me to open a betting account with some internet and phone betting organisation or something. I'm supposed to place bets on his horse in the race at Cheltenham. He put a large sum of money into my bank account to draw on."

"How large?" Vincent stood up. "How much money did he put into your account?" His voice became excited.

"Half a million pounds. I think he's going to try and bet all of it." She hesitated and felt herself blush. "Well not quite all of it. He's taken ten thousand pounds to book a trip for us to go away somewhere."

"And how do you go about getting this bet placed?" He ignored his wife's embarrassment.

"I go onto the internet, key in my password and register my bet. Andy says they e-mail confirmation that they've matched your bet, whatever that means."

"A betting exchange." Vincent looked down at her. "They find someone else who's registered with them who'll take your bet. If you win then the other person has to pay up but if you lose they keep your money. The betting exchange takes a commission from the bet. Quite simple really."

"Anyway, I'm supposed to put a sort of trial bet on today, five thousand pounds and let him know in the morning that I've done it."

"That's great." Vincent rubbed his hands together. "He's on the hook well and truly. Are you sure that he's only got ten thousand pounds. I mean he can't get his hands on the rest?"

"No it's in my bank account at Kingston he went with me and we put it in my account. Why's that important?"

"I made him a loan. He got the money from me and if it's in your bank I'd rather it stayed in the family, so to speak."

Miriam gasped. "Why on earth would you want to give him that amount of money? Come to that why would you give him any money at all especially if you know about," she hesitated and then said with a tremor in her voice, "well about him and me?"

"My dear, it's all part of my scheme to bring Andy Clewer down. Don Markham and I have worked it so that when I call in the loan he will lose his company to me. He'll have nothing. Don loathes him feels he should have some sort of share in the company so we're working together."

"Oh Vincent." She knew that Andy would be devastated. "No more fast cars. No more flash restaurants." A thought struck her. "But what about Suzanne - what will she do and how is Don involved?"

"Suzanne will be fine; I'm taking care of that." He shrugged his shoulders. "Don has felt cheated by Andy for years. He found out that Andy had been taking money from the company to fund his gambling and;" he gave his wife a rueful smile and sat down beside her, "his women. He came to me with an idea that would enable me to get my own back and him a share of the business."

"So you need to make sure that he can't get his hands on any more of the money otherwise he might be able to pay you back and that would ruin everything." She leaned toward him and taking his face in her hands kissed him gently on the lips.

He put his arms round her once more and returned her kiss with a passion. Finally pulling back he took both her hands in his. "Darling, I may not be the greatest lover in the book but I couldn't bear to lose you. If you want me to take you to restaurants like Bridgedale then I will. If you…"

Miriam placed her hand over his mouth. "Hush. I just want you. How could I have ever wanted anyone but you or anything else but your love."

"Miriam." Vincent's voice was thick with emotion. "Make love to me, please, right now."

She stood up and reached for his hand. "Come upstairs with me."

He pulled her back down to the sofa. "No. I mean let's make love here, now. On the sofa. On the floor. I don't mind but just let me feel you all around me."

He pulled her gently towards him. His lips nuzzled her neck and he whispered in her ear. "My darling, I'd be lost without you."

They sat together like that for several moments savouring the closeness of each other. She turned her face to his and they kissed - gently at first then with more urgency. Pushing her back in the sofa he slowly undid the buttons of her blouse, one by one telling her as each one came undone how much he loved her. Sliding his hand inside, he could feel the soft warm flesh of her breasts through the thin cotton of her bra.

"Let me help you." She breathed. Reaching behind her back she slipped the clasp and her breasts swung free in his hands.

He wasn't sure how it happened but all at once they were on the floor. He lay down beside her. "Oh Vincent my dear loving husband."

She whispered in his ear, her hands tugging at his belt. He slipped out of his trousers and pants, her hands caressing him all the time.

She raised herself up and with a few deft movements her skirt and panties were off and she was naked from the waist down.

She stroked his hair and kissed his forehead. She kissed each of his eyes in turn. She kissed the tip of his nose.

He let out a soft moan. "I can't take much more my darling angel." Sitting up he laid her back onto the soft carpet. She felt the weight of his body above her. With a gentle sigh he entered her. They rocked back and forward together and with a passionate cry he climaxed. "I'm sorry, I'm sorry." He whispered. "I couldn't hold back anymore."

She was crying. "Oh Vincent. That was wonderful. Please don't be sorry. Just lie here and hold me."

***

Andy checked his watch, just after 3.30. Might as well push off he thought to himself. Deciding not to go back to the office he fancied visiting the youth club in Croydon and headed off round the South Circular.

There were about a dozen young people in the Club when he arrived, several of them he recognised as being regulars at the time when he had previously visited.

"Hello Mr Clewer, nice to see you again," a young lad came over to shake his hand, "are you going to let me win at snooker this time?"

Andy laughed. "Randolph isn't it, yes I'll give you a game but I can only stay for an hour that should be time enough."

Having played a game with Randolph and lost Andy spent the next 25 minutes chatting with some of the youngsters before saying his goodbyes with a promise to call in more often.

He cursed the rush hour traffic on the M25 as he made his way round to the A3 toward Guildford and home.

It was difficult for Suzanne not to show her contempt for Andy when he breezed in that evening. Seemingly he had forgotten all about falling asleep in a drunken stupor.

"Supper ready?" He called as he started up the stairs. "Just going to get changed. I think I'll have a G & T. Plenty of ice there's a good girl."

"Plenty of arsenic if it's left to me." Suzanne spoke quietly to herself between gritted teeth. "You're home early." She called trying to keep her voice light. "Any special reason?"

"Do I need one to be home early and have a drink with my wife? I thought you'd be pleased. I'm going to have a shower. Be down soon."

Suzanne walked into the lounge, her mind a kaleidoscope of thoughts. She opened the drinks cabinet and took out the gin and a crystal tumbler. Pouring a healthy measure into the tumbler she went back to the kitchen. She took a couple of ice cubes from the freezer dropped them into the gin and topped up the glass up with tonic from the fridge. She hadn't thought about supper only about her talk with Vincent Floyd.

Poking around the freezer she found two pieces of salmon. She popped them onto a plate and into the microwave to defrost. In the fridge there were some new potatoes and purple sprouting broccoli. Also a bottle of Viognier. She poured herself a glass of the chilled white wine as she waited for the microwave to ping. That should do it with cheese to follow.

She scrubbed hard at the potatoes to release some of her anger and put them onto to boil. She placed a steamer basket on the top of the saucepan and washed the broccoli ready to put it into the steamer when the potatoes were nearly cooked.

Andy came into the room and put his arms round her. "Anything I can do to help?" Suzanne pulled away from him.

"You can lay the table in here while I cook the supper. Watch out I've got fishy fingers. I mean I've got fish on my hands – you know salmon." She smiled at the thought of Andy having fish fingers for tea.

"Knives and forks for the meal." Andy busied himself laying the table. "What's for afters?"

"I thought we'd have cheese and biscuits. Get the cheese out of the fridge. And Andy." He stopped and looked at her. "Don't forget the drink you ordered."

Humming to himself he missed the sarcasm in Miriam's words, finished laying the table, got out the plates and pulled the cork on a bottle of Australian Shiraz. "Thought that would go nicely with our cheese." He wandered across the kitchen and picked up his tumbler. "Cheers." He took a deep gulp of his drink. "Mmm that's good. What have you been up to?"

Suzanne pretended to concentrate on cooking the salmon so that he couldn't see her face as she lied to him. "Bit of window shopping in Kingston that's all."

"Kingston." Andy coughed and spluttered as the gin went down the wrong way. "Did you see anybody we know?" He managed to say between coughing and hiccupping.

"No, I wasn't there long. Just had a quick mooch round and then came back here to do a bit of tidying up. She added the last piece of broccoli to Andy's plate and turned from the stove. "Here we are."

They sat and ate their supper in the kitchen. Suzanne trying hard not to blurt out that she knew he was a double diamond, hundred carat, two timing deceiving rat and Andy trying not to show the relief he felt that he and Miriam hadn't been spotted.

When they had finished their cheese Suzanne began to load the dishwasher. As she bent forward to put the plates into the bottom tray Andy was behind her. A hand slid up the inside of her leg. She jumped and straightened up almost recoiling from his touch.

"Sorry, sweetheart, did I make you jump? He pulled her toward him and lowered his voice. "Let's go upstairs. You remember how you used to rub me with that oil of yours. Well I feel so horny and if you rub me all over I'll make sure that you get all the jumping you need." He laughed at his own joke as he tried to take her hand. "I'll make up for the other night; you know when I fell asleep. Feel how excited I am."

Pulling away from him she turned back to the dirty plates on the work top above the dishwasher. "Not tonight Andy, I really am quite tired. I think I'll just read a book, take a tablet and get a good night's sleep. I think you'd better take another shower and perhaps sleep in the spare room, don't you?"

She slammed shut the door to the dishwasher and walked out of the kitchen leaving him standing there lost for words.

Chapter 18

Andy hadn't slept well. His mind whirling with thoughts of huge winning bets had kept him awake and he was up by 6.30am. He sat in his dressing gown in the kitchen drinking coffee wondering what odds Miriam had managed to get and how much she'd wagered. He'd told her to bet five thousand pounds. He just hoped the silly cow hadn't tried to put too much on as that would start alarm bells ringing at the betting exchange.

He knew that they monitored the pattern of bets and could put a halt to any bets that they thought might be manipulated or orchestrated to any degree. Not only that but they would alert the police. Finding a couple of slices of bread he made himself some toast.

At 7 o'clock he poured a coffee for Suzanne and took it up to the bedroom. He put the cup onto the bedside table and gently shook her shoulder. She was lying on her side and was wearing one of the eye masks that are dished out to first and business class passengers on long haul flights.

"It's just gone seven and I'm off to the office once I've had a shave and got dressed. There's a coffee here for you." She struggled to sit up in bed, pulling off the eye mask and scrunching her pillow up against the headboard she reached for the coffee.

He walked into the en-suite and plugging in his electric razor started to shave. "Take my blue pin-stripe suit to the cleaners." He shouted above the buzz of the razor. "And we need some more bread."

"Yes master." Suzanne knew he couldn't hear her through the noise of his razor. He finished shaving and she could hear the water running as he brushed his teeth.

"Did you hear me?" He strode across the bedroom, opened his wardrobe and selected a shirt.

"Yes. We need bread and please will I take your suit to the cleaners I think that's what you said."

"No need to be sarcastic Suzanne." He buttoned up his shirt and reached for his trousers. "After the way you treated me last night

I would have thought you'd have been saying sorry." He sat on the edge of the bed to pull on his loafers. "Anyway I'm not going to argue with you I've got to go. I'm not sure what time I'll be in tonight."

He stood and pulling a jacket from its hanger moved toward the door stopping with one hand on the door handle. "Don't forget that suit. I'll want it for the races next week."

She heard him go down the stairs and out of the door. She sat and listened to his car start and then move out of the garage and down the drive. "You selfish, selfish bastard." The words come out full of bitterness and she felt the prickle of tears in her eyes.

***

Miriam and Vincent had breakfast together. He liked porridge with honey and she had taken extra care to see that it was just the way he liked it.

"You'll have to ring Andy later this morning you know." Vincent spoke between spoonfuls of porridge. "He'll be expecting it."

"But I haven't put his bet on." Miriam looked at her husband her eyes wide. "If he knows that I'm not sure what he'll do."

"You're not going to put his bet on. He'll never know if you have or not so there's no need for you to worry." He raised his eyebrows. "Anyway, it's not his money to bet, it's in your account not his."

"You mean I tell him the bet's on but I don't really do anything but what if asks questions you know like how much will he get?"

"That's right. You tell him you've managed to get the five thousand pounds placed at odds of 3-1. That should keep him happy. Now my dear, I must make a move and get into the office. Make sure you keep busy and out of Clewer's way." He gave a gentle smile. "Can you do that?"

"Oh yes. I'm not going near him ever again you can be sure of that don't you worry."

"Oh but you'll have to. Don't forget we're going racing with him and Suzanne next week." Wiping his mouth on his napkin he stood and moved away from the table. "Give me a call if you need me. I'll see you tonight about sixish. I love you."

Miriam jumped up and moved hurriedly round the table. Putting her arms around him she kissed him tenderly. "I love you to. Do you think I should give Suzanne a ring?"

"Why not. It's better to talk to her now, not wait until the races. Have lunch with her - ask her over here. Clear the air now and then you can both enjoy watching him squirm."

***

Andy walked into his office just after 8.15. Debbie was already at her desk and sorting through the post.

"Morning Debbie. And how's my little sex pot this morning." Andy leaned on her desk and stretched his face toward her. "Got a little kiss for me?"

She leaned forward and their lips briefly touched. "I've got to finish the minutes of the board meeting Andy. Don wants to approve them before lunch so they can be circulated."

"But you've got time to get your boss a cup of coffee." Andy turned and walked into his office.

He was behind his desk when she came in carrying a tray with his cup and a plate of biscuits.

"Why don't you close the door? We've got twenty minutes or so before the others get in." He grinned. "I fancy you like mad this morning."

She pulled a face. "Not this morning Andy; I can't you know." She looked at him and wondered. How could I think he'd ever want me for anything else but sex? "Sorry."

She picked up the tray and opening the door turned to him. "Do you want the door leaving open?"

"Might as well." Miriam's phone call, the thought struck him. "No on second thoughts close it. I need some peace and quiet this morning." He waved her away.

His mobile rang at 9.15. He snatched it up and pressed the button to receive the call. "Clewer." He snapped. "Oh it's you. You took your time. Is the bet on?"

He listened intently. "Not bad for a start. We need to get more on next time. We'll try for ten thousand but we won't push it. Meet me at that Italian restaurant in Bentalls, you know the place we went to before and we can put the bet on across the road in that internet café I'll see you about 10 o'clock. He paused. "And Miriam, don't forget to bring the password this time."

His face darkened as he heard her make excuses. "Can't you bloody well get out of it. Lunch with a girlfriend comes a poor second to getting this bet on. You need to get your priorities sorted." Miriam's voice replied with a firmness that was new to him and he slammed his mobile down on the desk so hard that the case split. "Bollocks. What's the matter with the women in my life? None of them can do as they're told."

Debbie had heard the ring of his mobile and strained her ears to hear the conversation. His raised voice carried through the closed door of his office. Debbie looked up and smiled. Oh dear, not getting his own way today. That makes a change she thought.

***

Phoning Suzanne to invite her over hadn't been that difficult once she'd plucked up the courage to do it. There had been no shouting or screaming as she'd expected. In fact on reflection Suzanne had accepted the invitation with calm resignation. But now the butterflies were working overtime in Miriam's stomach as she waited for the door-bell to ring. She'd heard a car pull up in the drive and stood looking nervously at the inside of the front door.

When it did ring it made her start. Taking a deep breath she turned the latch and pulled the door open wide. "Suzanne." It was all she could say before the tears cascaded down her face.

Closing the door behind her Suzanne took hold of Miriam's hands. "Don't Miriam." Her voice was harsh. "He's not worth it. If it hadn't been you it would have been someone else. In fact there has always been someone else. There was someone at the same time as you so he cheated on us both."

Miriam allowed herself to be led into the kitchen, her mind racing. He was two timing her. "I'm sorry Suzanne, so sorry for what I've done." She sniffed back her tears. "But Vincent's got a plan. Can we work together?"

"I'm not sure. It really hurt to know that you of all people, my friend, had …" Suzanne's face twisted as it was her turn to fight back the tears. "Well you know what you did. Nobody more than me wants to see him get what he deserves." There was a steely edge to her voice. "For years now he's ignored me, you know, as a woman. Oh I've been useful for entertaining his business contacts, being the dutiful little wife, putting in appearances at corporate functions."

Bitterness crept into her voice. "But anything physical finished years ago." She felt Miriam stiffen at her words. "Nothing to do with you my dear, long before you. We've both been taken in by him." She took a deep breath. "I'm willing to forget just so that I can get even with him. Who knows maybe in time we could be friends again."

Miriam felt her spirits lift. "I'd like that. But what did you mean there was someone else?"

"His secretary Debbie. He was screwing her at every opportunity. Always greedy our Andy one woman would never satisfy him. Before her it was some girl at the stables. Suzanne grimaced. "I found out what he meant when he used to tell me he was going for a ride. Look let's just concentrate on making sure he doesn't suspect anything and wait for the rug to be pulled from under him."

"Do you know Suzanne I'd like to drink to that. There's a pub just down the road and they've got a superb lunchtime menu." Eagerly Miriam stood up. "Come on let's go and eat."

The ringing of the phone stopped them both dead in their tracks. "It might be Andy." The light hearted spring had gone from Miriam's tread as she moved to pick up the phone.

She smiled as she listened to the voice on the other end. "Just a minute." She put her hand over the receiver. "It's Vincent he wants to meet us for lunch." She moved her hand. "I was just telling Suzanne who it was. We're going to the Golden Lion can you meet us there? Ok, see you shortly." She hung up and turned excitedly to Suzanne. "He says he has some news."

The two women walked the half mile to the pub. They were in luck for as it was early they had the pick of the tables. Choosing one tucked into a corner they sat down and ordered a bottle of wine.

When it arrived Suzanne poured them both a glass. "Here's to getting even." They clinked glasses, taking a sip of wine before picking up and studying the menu.

"Hello you two." Vincent stood looking from one woman to the other. Everything OK - I mean between the two of you?"

"We're going to be fine, aren't we Suzanne?" His wife smiled up at him. "Make yourself useful there's a dear, see what the soup of the day is and then come and tell us your news."

"Hang on there, let a man get a drink will you you're ahead of me." He grinned and turning strode to the bar.

In a few minutes he was back with a pint of Young's Special. "Celeriac and stilton is today's soup. Recommended by the young lady behind the bar."

"That sounds good, what about you?" Suzanne nodded. "Me too. Be an angel Vincent, go and order." Miriam pouted at him.

"Righto - that's three soups then." He stood up and went over to the bar. He was back a few moments later clutching a small stand with the number six on top.

"They'll call our number when it's ready. About five or so minutes she said. He sat down and picked up his beer. "Cheers. At last I was gasping." The two woman raised their glasses as he took a deep gulp of his beer. "That's better."

"What's this news then? Miriam sat forward on her seat. "Is it to do with Andy's bet?

"No, it's to do with Suzanne." He turned toward her. "I've had my solicitors talking to the bank on your behalf and set the wheels in motion to get the house back for you."

"That's wonderful." Suzanne gasped as a thought struck her. "Won't Andy need to be involved in sorting out the paperwork?"

"No as the house was in your name and the solicitors said they were acting for you so he's not involved in any way and all..."

"Number six – number six." The girl from behind the bar called interrupting Vincent.

"Over here." He waved the number over his head. "I'll finish telling when we've been served."

Moments later with a basket of freshly baked crusty bread set in the middle of the table and bowls of steaming soup in front of each of them Vincent continued.

"Hope you're free on Monday morning Suzanne. I've arranged for the papers assigning the deeds of the house to the bank to be brought round to my solicitors' office. They'll need your signature and one or two other formalities to be completed and the deeds will be back with you, don't worry, they'll explain everything to you."

Her face lit up. "Vincent words, fail me. That's really marvellous." She stopped and stared at him. "He won't be able to get it away from me will he?"

"Once everything's sorted out with the bank just leave the deeds with my solicitors for safekeeping. He can't get at them there." He picked up a piece of bread and spread it with a generous of portion of butter. "Now come on eat up while the soup's still hot."

"You know Vincent, when this is all over I'm going to sell the house and pay you back." Suzanne nodded. "I'll find myself a nice flat somewhere. It'll be good to make a fresh start away from it all."

Vincent patted her hand in a kindly way. "All in good time my dear, all in good time."

Chapter 19

Andy had managed a quick trip to the stables and he and Adrian were in the tack room talking to Cowboy, Adrian's travelling head lad. The tack room was Cowboy's domain. Sorting through the battered wardrobe that stood along one wall he pulled out a hanger.

"I've got your silks ready washed Mr Clewer." He held up the hanger.

"Just see that you keep them that way I want Wayne to look good." Andy grunted and turned to Adrian. "When does the horse leave for Cheltenham?"

"There's no need to go up the night before so Cowboy will be leaving at 9.00 on race morning. It should take a couple of hours in the box to get up to there. The horse only needs to be there at least forty five minutes before the race off time but I always leave plenty of time for emergencies. Cut it too fine and there's a problem with the traffic or a breakdown, you're stuffed. Besides which I want to give him a chance to settle after the journey."

"He's out in the yard Boss." Jonny, the assistant trainer, stuck his head through the tack room door.

"Come on then let's go and look at your boy." Adrian led the way out into the early morning dampness leaving Cowboy in the tack room sorting through a tangle of silks straight out of the washing machine.

The horse walked in a steady rolling gait round the circle of grass in the middle of the stable yard. Adrian stood with Andy beside him, his critical eye missing nothing as Alternative Ways snorted and whinnied his way round. Every now and then gave a little jig, bouncing on his toes causing the lad leading him round to lean back on the rein to steady him.

"He looks alright to me." Andy tilted his head this way and that, trying to see if he could spot anything wrong with the way the horse was walking.

Jonny had gone back to weighing out the feed for the next lot coming back from the gallops and they were standing on their own with their backs against AW's loose box. "I know he looks OK. The lameness has gone so he walks OK but that's not the problem."

"What do you mean 'that's not the problem' – what is the problem? Andy's face darkened. "You are going to run him Adrian, aren't you?"

Adrian rubbed the side of his face. "It's just that he needs at least another week of fast work to put him spot on but the race is only two days away."

"So what's this problem?" Andy with a face like thunder jabbed Adrian's arm to emphasise his words.

"What I mean is without that extra week's work he won't be as fit as I would like." He looked flustered. "He's still favourite in the ante-post betting but if word got out it would…."

"But word isn't going to get out." Andy snapped cutting him short. "I've backed the horse to the hilt. Remember you're going to get your share when the horse loses so don't start getting cold feet." He slapped Adrian on the back. "We're in this together so just make sure that everything stays normal – alright?"

"Alright." Adrian gave a weak smile. "I'm just really gutted at the thought of the lads and lasses in the yard who've already put their cash on him. Probably even borrowed money to put their bets on. It just doesn't seem fair somehow."

"Not fair." Andy snarled. "I'll tell you what's not bloody fair. An owner spending cartloads of money to keep a horse in training and just when he gets the chance to hit the good times with a big win – the bloody horse gets knackered."

"I know all of that." Adrian retaliated. "But you've got the money they haven't. It means such a lot to them."

"It means a bloody lot to me." Andy's voice had got louder as his temper increased. "You can always give them some money from your pay back if you feel that bothered about it."

"Did you call, Boss?" One of the lads leaned out from a loose box further down the yard.

"No, carry on." Adrian waved his hand at the lad who, with a shrug of his shoulders disappeared back inside.

"You see I haven't got the money." Looking round Andy kept his voice low and spoke in a threatening tone. "If my backing him to lose doesn't come off I'm finished. So don't talk to me about what it means to other people. Got me."

"OK, OK. It's just I'm a bit on edge. If the Jockey Club found out then I'd be the one who's finished."

"You get the horse to the meeting looking as good as he does today and nobody will blame you when he loses. I'll see you on Thursday at the meeting, come up to the box and have a drink. If there any problems give me a call." Without waiting for a reply he turned and walked back to his parked his car.

Driving back to his office he used the car phone to ring Miriam. His mood wasn't improved when all he got was the answer phone.

He stormed into his office. "Debbie give me a run-down of the arrangements for Saturday. I suppose you have done them."

Pulling a face behind his back Debbie opened a drawer in her desk and took out a folder.

She carried it through to his office. "The car will pick you and Suzanne up at 8.00am. You'll go on to Richmond to collect Vincent Floyd and his wife. Don and his partner are picking the Swedes up from their hotel, they're staying at La Cuisine by the way and George Nicol and his wife will make their own way there. You're meeting at La Cuisine at 9.15 for breakfast and the box at the racecourse is available from 11.00. They'll start serving lunch at twelve thirty and..."

"Have you made sure that the cars have car park labels?" He interrupted. "I don't want to be embarrassed by none of the cars being let into the owners' car park."

"You've already got your Racehorse Owners pass. I've got a label for Don and I've sent one to George Nicol's office with a map for his driver. Everyone has an itinerary and timetable."

"The caterers know who we are. I mean that they've got to be on their toes I only want top class service so no pimply faced kids trying to serve."

"I'm sure they will. I've checked with everyone and nobody has any dietary problems so the menu you chose is fine. They're putting a dozen bottles of vintage champagne on ice. Anyway I'll be there to make sure it all goes smoothly."

"Pol Roger? Andy leaned back in his chair. "The champagne I mean, it's got to be Pol Roger."

"They'll serve afternoon tea at 3 o'clock." Debbie ignored him. "And drinks and snacks will be available all day. That just about covers it."

"Right. Get back to work now I need to make some calls." Andy busied himself getting his mobile phone from his briefcase and missed the look on Debbie's face at her curt dismissal.

She flounced her way across the office. "And Debbie" She turned. "Close the door on your way out." It made her feel better to slam the door so hard that the frame shook.

He tried Miriam again. Her mobile rang until it went into the messaging service and when he tried the home phone again he still got the answer phone.

He got up and paced backwards and forwards. "Bloody woman – what the hell's she playing at."

***

Miriam phoned her husband at the office. "He's called three times now Vincent, I'm worried he might come round."

"Call him on his mobile and tell him that you're at that, oh you know, that, what's its name spa place."

"You mean the Parkside Country Club, they do an amazing facial with exfoliating and hydrating."

"That's it". Vincent interrupted. I don't need the full list just tell him you're on an all-day treatment getting yourself pampered ready for the big race day. Tell him you've got another bet on and not to worry you'll get the next one on tomorrow."

"I'll go to the Parkside for lunch. I can take my book and sit in the relaxation area. You won't be late home, darling, will you?"

"Why don't I pick you up at the spa and we can go and have some supper together. About 6 o'clock. We could go up to town."

"I'd like that. Yes pick me up there. I'll take a change of clothes with me. You could try for the Maze. You can get an assortment of tasters, not just one dish. I rather fancy that - a little bit of everything."

Laughing, Vincent rang off leaving his wife to book herself into the Parkside for the rest of the day.

***

Andy had left early that morning to go to the stables which suited Suzanne as she had another appointment with Vincent's solicitors up in London. She caught the train from Guildford arriving into Waterloo just after 10 o'clock.

Snodbury, Turner and Partners had their offices in Westminster Bridge Road which was a short walk from the station and it didn't take long before she was standing in the solicitor's reception area waiting for Clarence Turner himself to see her.

Moments later his secretary guided her upstairs and into a spacious, airy office with large picture windows on two sides and from one there was a glimpse of the River Thames.

Clarence Turner stood up from behind his desk. "Mrs Clewer, please come in and sit down. Janice will get us some coffee."

"Yes thank you." Suzanne felt nervous as she sat down in the leather armchair. On the other side of a small regency style coffee table was its twin. "Mr Turner, you know the situation I'm in. I'm not certain what I've signed and how it can be sorted. When we last met you said you would explain everything to me."

"Of course my dear." Turner nodded kindly. "But let's have some coffee while we talk." Janice poured coffee for them both and quietly closed the door as she left the room.

"Your husband put the family house in your name – most probably for tax purposes."

He picked up a file from his desk and took out a bound sheath of papers. Sitting down opposite Suzanne he pulled a pair of half-moon spectacles from his jacket pocket and perched them on the end of his nose.

"Now let me see." He glanced down at the bundle. "In September 2000 he borrowed seventy five thousand pounds and pledged shares in his company as security." The thick paper made a dry rustling noise as he turned the pages. "In 2002 he redeemed his shares, borrowed a further five hundred thousand using the house as surety. He took off his glasses and looked at Suzanne. "And that's when you signed a deed of assignment which meant that if the money is not paid back – well quite simply, my dear, the house belongs to the bank."

"Just like that." She blurted out a look of horror on her face. "I mean he can actually do that?"

He spread the bundle open on the table between them. "That is your signature Mrs Clewer?"

Suzanne peered at the page where his finger pointed to a signature next to an official stamp. Turning the bundle round to get a better look she nodded. "Yes."

"So as far as the bank's concerned you've given your consent for, what in name is your property, to be used to secure Mr Clewer's loan. Anyway, the point is that the appropriate sum of money has been lodged with the bank and we are now able to get them to re-assign the property back to you." He paused and turned the bundle round and leafed through the pages. "Here we are. If you sign here and…." Turning the page. "Here - I've got the deeds in the strong room and you can take them with you."

"Could you keep them for me Mr Turner?" Suzanne leaned forward. "I don't want my husband to be able to get his hands on them again. I'd be much happier if they stayed here."

"Of course Mrs Clewer that'll be no problem. So that we can act on your behalf and retain documents for you I must ask you to sign our client arrangement agreement." He held up both hands. "Bureaucracy, I'm afraid. But it safeguards us both against fraud."

Twenty minutes later Suzanne left the offices of Snodbury, Turner and Partners feeling elated that, with the help of Vincent Floyd, she had at last started to get even with her conniving husband.

In the train on the way back to Guildford she tried to imagine the look on Andy's face when he found out that the house was back in her name. Her lips twitched in a smile, her house and nothing he could do.

***

There was a strict rule at the Parkside Country Club and Spa that mobile phones were to be switched off before entering the building. If you wanted to be contacted it had to be through the Spa's reception where messages could be left. There was a business centre with telephones, online computers and other office facilities for guests to use during their stay. The membership fees were astronomical but all-inclusive and ensured complete privacy if one desired.

Miriam was confident that Andy would not be able to reach her even if he did find out where she had gone. She was looking forward to a day of relaxation and pampering.

"Good morning Mrs Floyd." The receptionist greeted her with a warm smile and looked down at the day's register showing on her screen. "We've got you down for the full body massage later this morning, lunch in the conservatory and manicure and facial this afternoon."

"Sounds good. Have I got time for a swim before the massage…?" Miriam looked at the girls name badge pinned to the lapel of her bottle green blazer. "Katie?"

"Plenty of time Mrs Floyd. You're booked in for 11.30 and there's not many swimming today."

Smiling her thanks Miriam made her way through to the ladies locker and shower room. Taking her time she undressed and put on a one piece bathing costume. Into a small shoulder bag she put the novel she was reading, her purse and moisturiser. She took a quick shower and with the bag in one hand walked through the door to the swimming pool area.

The pool was designed for relaxation rather than exercise and had cushioned sun loungers arranged down either side. Each one placed discreet distance from the next so as to maintain a level of privacy. Fluffy bottle green folded bath sheets were piled up on tables as you left the locker room. Taking two, Miriam set them out on the lounger she selected and slipping off the beach shoes she was wearing got ready for a swim.

The water was about the same temperature as the Arabian Gulf, around 25° centigrade, and as she floated on her back she felt the tension and stress of the last few days slip away. Kicking her legs gently she moved slowly down the pool to the end. The depth was an even one and a half metres all the way. Turning over she swam with a lazy breaststroke back to the other end. Getting out she walked to her lounger and towelled herself dry before settling down on the soft cushions to read her book.

Fed up with reading after half an hour, she ordered coffee and propped up the back of the lounger when it arrived so that she could sit in comfort. Sipping at her coffee she gazed round, her mind drifting. Through the windows that ranged down one side of the pool, for one fleeting moment she recognised the shape of an Aston Martin as it drove from the gates into the Club grounds. Her hand shook spilling coffee onto her legs and the bath sheet beneath. Only one thought invaded her mind – Andy Clewer had found her. Panic galvanised her into action. Pushing the cup and saucer under the lounger she jumped up and grabbed her book and bag. She ran toward the ladies locker room drawing puzzled glances from the few other people round the pool.

Once in the locker room she sat down, her chest heaving and heart thumping as if she'd just run a hundred metres. I'm safe in here she thought. He won't be allowed into the ladies changing rooms – but with Andy she knew she couldn't be sure.

The door from reception crashed open. Miriam shrank back against her locker trying to make herself invisible. Two ladies walked in both wearing designer track suits and enough gold jewellery to cover the debt of a small nation. They were talking loudly complaining about the size of the parking spaces. It was then that she realised the Aston Martin was theirs and not Andy's. She felt so foolish and didn't relish the idea of going back to the pool area. The clock over the door told her that there was only ten minutes to her first treatment session.

Stripping off her costume she opened up her locker and having towelled herself dry, pulled on a bikini. Bath robes were supplied for all guests and she slipped one on. Putting her wet costume in the locker she closed and locked the door, gathered up her book and bag and set off for the massage room. Within a few minutes she was being welcomed by the masseuse and again felt a sense of calm wellbeing drift over her as the aromatic oils were applied to her body with firm but gentle hands. She thought of the evening ahead and was glad that Vincent had suggested going out for supper.

Chapter 20

The cars that Debbie had hired to pick up Andy and his guests were Mercedes Sprinter vans skilfully converted into people carriers adapted to provide executive luxury for the passengers. With four pairs of mid-grey leather swivel armchairs, each pair having their own table, all were within easy reach of a small fridge and drinks cabinet. Each armchair had its own individual reading light and could be eased back into a reclining position if desired. The floor was finished with a deep pile maroon wool carpet and the windows had a tint that prevented anyone outside from seeing in. As there were only 4 travelling in the luxurious interior the armchairs had been adjusted so that four of the chairs were round one table.

"Bloody hell Suzanne hurry up, slapping on a bit of make-up can't take that long surely," Andy bellowed up the stairs, "The car will be here soon."

Suzanne sat at her dressing table and applied a touch more foundation to her face with a soft make up brush. "Brian will have to wait." She pursed her lips as she ran the lipstick over them. "You want me to look at my best don't you? After all we'll be on the TV when we receive the prize."

"Yes alright but get a move on will you it isn't as if the war paint will make any difference. And let's face it that outfit you're wearing doesn't do a lot for the well-padded woman. In fact maybe I should have Miriam with me to collect the prize." Laughing to himself he picked up the Racing Post and read the headline for the third time since the papers had been delivered ten minutes earlier. 'WHICHEVER WAY YOU BET – MAKE IT ALTERNATIVE.' the favourite to romp home in a quality field.

Upstairs Suzanne smiled. If only you knew she thought to herself. Humming the old Frank Sinatra classic, 'I did it my way'; she shrugged into her full, hand knitted cashmere coat. She perched a matching hat onto her head, smoothed down her hair and with a quick check in the mirror set off down the stairs.

As she reached the bottom the doorbell rang. Opening it Brian, Andy's chauffeur, stood there.

Suzanne stuck her head out through the open door. "Hello Brian - gosh it's cold. I see you're flattering the boss." She nodded at his tie coloured with navy blue and emerald green diamonds that matched Andy's racing colours.

"Morning Mrs Clewer, that's right." Brian nodded respectfully and touched the tie. "The car's nice and warm so you won't be needing your coat on. I've checked the forecast and it's going to be cold but bright."

"Don't stand there chatting up my wife, Brian." Andy snapped as he stormed past, a dark overcoat over his arm and a brown trilby in his hand. "I pay you to drive not to chat." He walked toward the gleaming Mercedes that Brian had parked adjacent to the front door.

"Sorry Mr Clewer." Brian ran to get in front of his boss so that he could slide the door open. Andy grunted as he got in, selected a seat and slumped down into the sumptuous rear passenger compartment.

Glaring at his wife he leaned forward. "Well, get a bloody move on. Shut the front door and get your arse over here." He paused, patting the pockets of his coat. "No wait a minute. Get my binoculars I've left them on the kitchen table."

"I'll go, Mrs Clewer." Brian looked embarrassed at the way Andy was shouting at his wife. "You get into the warm." He helped Suzanne through the door and left her to settle herself as he moved quickly to find Andy's binoculars.

Within a few minutes the house was locked up, Andy's binoculars were on his lap and the car was crunching its way down the drive. At that time on a Saturday morning it didn't take long to reach the A3 and head toward Richmond.

Using his mobile Andy rang to let Vincent know they were on their way and then settled back to read the Racing Post. Brian kept the car moving at a steady seventy miles an hour along the dual carriageway only slowing where the speed limit required it. Twenty minutes later they were turning off the A3 onto Roehampton Lane and then into the Richmond Deer Park.

Vincent and Miriam were ready and waiting and as the car pulled up they came out of the house. Brian jumped out of the car the moment he had brought it to a stop. "Morning Mr and Mrs Floyd." He pulled open the door and stood back as they got in.

"Sit next to me Miriam." Andy patted the grey leather seat next to his. "I'll give you a few tips."

"Why don't you give me a few tips instead?" Vincent Floyd eased himself into the seat next to Andy. "Let the girls have time to catch up on what they've been up to." He smiled fondly at his wife. "Tell Suzanne all about your day at the Parkside."

Miriam sank down in her seat and nodded. "Yes Suzanne I must tell you they've got a new masseuse – she's really very good."

Brian slid the door closed and went round the car and got in behind the wheel. All set Mr Clewer?" He turned and looked over his shoulder at Andy.

"Just get on and drive Brian." He leaned forward. "Did you put the champagne in the fridge as I told you?"

"All there Mr Clewer." Brian concentrated on easing the car out into the traffic of the South Circular as they made their way to the M4 and on toward Oxford.

"A glass of champagne for anyone?" Andy looked at his travelling companions as they each shook their heads. "Bloody miserable lot – better wait I suppose, no point in drinking on my own. We're stopping at that French hotel on the way for breakfast La Cuisine it's called' we can have champagne then." He leaned back and stared morosely out of the window at the passing countryside.

Brian had put four copies of the Racing Post on the table in the car. Vincent had picked up a copy and was studying the runners and riders of the day's racing. Suzanne and Miriam had their heads together and were chatting quite happily.

Andy sat there alone with his thoughts only the tightness of his clenched jaw gave any outward sign of the tension he was feeling as they headed off. He glanced down at the lead article in the paper. 'Nothing to stop Alternative Ways becoming the country's leading chaser' read the first line. 'Victory today must be assured based on his performance at Uttoxeter.' The confidence of the author of the lead article did nothing to ease his tension. He desperately needed to know how much in total Miriam had managed to bet. No wonder he hadn't been able to speak with the silly bitch the other day she'd been closeted in some health spa. For her sake she'd better have wagered a fair amount of money or else he'd...

Vincent's voice interrupted his thoughts. "Your boy looks red hot to win today." He tapped the paper. "They're all tipping him."

"Yeah - well he's still got some decent horses to beat." He gave a grimace. "Nothing is that certain in racing you know."

"I can just see you and Suzanne in the winner's enclosure." Vincent smiled at her across the table. "You look really nice my dear, the TV cameras are bound to home in on you."

"Andy doesn't think so. Do you Andy?" Her face twisted into a grin as she saw her husband struggle to answer. "He told me so this morning. What was it about well-padded women?"

"Just a joke dear." He gave a half-hearted laugh. "I was trying to hurry you up. Oh look we're nearly there and at last I'll be able to have a drink."

Leaving the main road Brian drove down a narrow lane before turning between two brick pillars each topped with a sandstone statue in the shape of a griffin.

"Looks like Don's already here." Andy leaned forward in his seat to peer over Brian's shoulder at an identical Mercedes parked beside the entrance to La Cuisine. "Breakfast in the...." He pulled a piece of paper from his pocket and glanced at it. "Garden Room, that's if that bloody secretary of mine has done her job properly."

"My, my you are grumpy this morning, leave poor Debbie alone." Suzanne pulled a face. "Get out of bed the wrong side, did we?"

As if on cue Debbie appeared and waved at them from the doorway of the hotel to greet them. Andy frowned at his wife and stepped down from the car. "Everybody here, Debbie?"

"George Nicol's about five minutes away and Don and the Swedes are already into the coffee. Morning Mrs Clewer, Mr and Mrs Vincent; if you follow me I'll show you the way."

As Suzanne walked past him, Andy grabbed her hand. Not used to her standing up for herself he was put out by her flippant manner.

"What are you playing at?" He hissed his voice low and menacing. "Don't try and show me up in front of Floyd and his wife – I don't like it."

"Sorry darling." Suzanne realised that she needed to act normally or else he would get suspicious. "I'm just excited; you know looking forward to the race. Come on let's get some breakfast." She pulled away from him and followed the others into the hotel leaving Andy to trail along behind with a scowl on his face.

The Garden Room was light and airy with a cheerful log fire crackling in the hearth. A large round table was set with silver cutlery and there was a buffet bar down one side of the room with hot and cold food hidden under vast stainless steel lids. The Swedes and Don stood looking out of the French windows onto a vista of sweeping lawns with carefully trimmed shrubs and well-kept flower beds.

Andy hurried over to greet Marcus Carlson the managing director of the Swedish company and his wife Helena. As well as the Carlsons there were Lennart and Ulla Sandvik from Sweden. Lennart was the marketing director and it was his innovative ideas that had boosted sales of alternative medicines in the Scandinavian countries. Debbie made sure that everyone was armed with coffee and tea as the introductions were made ushering in waiters armed with silver pots and bone china cups and saucers. There were more introductions to be made when the Nicols arrived and talk became more animated as they discussed the day ahead.

Andy clapped his hands to gain attention. "If you'd like to help yourselves from the buffet everyone we should get breakfast started. I thought Bucks Fizz would go down well and start the day off on the right foot. Debbie make sure everybody is well looked after."

Before long they were all seated at the table with plates of smoked salmon, scrambled eggs and grilled tomatoes. Crystal flutes sparkled with champagne and orange juice as they raised their glasses to toast their host and success at the races.

Debbie, Brian and the Nicol's driver had a more subdued breakfast in the hotel dining room; although Debbie made sure she had a glass of champagne. Brian, who couldn't drink because he was driving, made up for it by having seconds of bacon and sausage.

By 10.30 they were all back in the cars and heading across country to Cheltenham. Debbie had left her car at the hotel and was sitting next to Brian. Andy had opened a bottle and the four passengers in the back sat sipping the chilled champagne as they watched fields with cattle and sheep grazing separated by green hedgerows pass by.

They had re-joined the M40 motorway and on reaching junction eight had turned onto the A40, bypassing Oxford as they headed toward Cheltenham. The racecourse was outside of Cheltenham itself just off the main road to Evesham and the countryside soon gave way to the sprawling outskirts of the town. As they neared the course the traffic was almost at a standstill. Coaches full of eager race goers, anxious to get to the course and the beer tents stretched endlessly in front of them interspersed with cars which left no opportunity for overtaking. The vehicles combined to create an almighty traffic jam on the approaches to the course. Andy sat forward on the edge of his seat.

"Any way round this Brian, I've got to meet Adrian." He looked round at the others. "Talk tactics and that sort of thing."

"Sorry Mr Clewer." Brian half turned his head but kept his eyes on the stationary traffic in front of them. "It'll be the same whichever way we go." Andy sat back with a sigh, only the whiteness of his knuckles as they gripped the edge of the table betrayed the feeling of frustration that was building inside.

Chapter 21

It was just before midday when Brian finally pulled up beside the owners' and trainers' entrance at Prestbury Park, Cheltenham's racecourse. He got out and opened the rear door.

"I'll be waiting for you here after the last race Mr Clewer. If there's any change to your plans Debbie can give me a call on my mobile." He nodded his head toward her as she scurried toward the owners' entrance.

"Get yourself some lunch, Brian." Andy pulled a twenty pound note from his pocket. "Give us half an hour after the last race, let some of the traffic go."

Brian nodded as he slid the door shut. "Will do, thanks Mr Clewer, good luck everyone."

Suzanne had wrapped herself in her cashmere coat. "God, that wind's cold. Can't we get inside?"

Debbie was standing by the gate to the course armed with a handful of entrance badges. "Over here. I've got a race card for everybody."

They trooped over collecting their badges and race cards from Debbie as they went through the gate and into the exclusive club enclosure. "Just head toward the grandstand. Take the lift to the third floor; our box is marked Alternative Ways in honour of our red hot favourite."

"I'll just go and see if Adrian's in the owners' bar. Anyone want to come with me – Miriam?" Andy looked at her his eyebrows raised.

"No it's too cold I'll go straight up to the box." Miriam pulled the collar of her coat up around her neck.

Andy turned away, a scowl on his face and set off toward the marquee set aside for owners and trainers. He was desperate to find out how much money she had bet. The marquee was packed but he couldn't see any sign of his trainer. His mood darkened and by the time he made his way back to the box in the grandstand he struggled to put a smile on his face as he strode in.

"Can't find the bloody man." He announced. "He's probably down at the stables checking on the horse, I'll catch him later. Everyone got a drink?" He snapped his fingers at the girl dressed in a white blouse, dark skirt and wearing a small apron. "Make sure everyone has champagne and keep them filled – we're here to celebrate." His voice held a confidence that he didn't feel.

Andy wandered through the sliding doors at the front of the box and out onto the balcony. He was finding it harder and harder to keep still, his thoughts constantly turning to Miriam and his bet. Marcus Carlson joined him.

"In Sweden we have mainly trotting races."

"Trotting races – what. Oh sorry Marcus I was miles away." Andy pulled himself out of his reverie. "Yes I know what you mean but I think you'll find this more exciting."

"What will we find more exciting?" Vincent had moved out onto the balcony. "Something else up your sleeve Clewer?"

Andy looked at his watch. "As a matter of fact there is. Come on inside and you'll see." He ushered the two men back into the warmth of the box and slid the door closed.

"Is he here yet?" He raised his eyebrows toward Debbie. As if on cue the door opened and a larger than life figure almost bounced in. "Hello everyone." The voice and face were familiar to anyone who watched the early morning racing channel. "I've just got a few minutes to run through the race card with you and help you make a few bob." His loud laugh rattled round the room. Pete McIlroy had arrived.

"Race cards ready and here we go." The pundit briefly analysed each race. Giving his view of each of the runners, their strengths and weaknesses he suggested which he thought would win. He left the XYZ Handicap Chase until last. He turned to Andy. "Now your boy looks the bet of the day. He fairly romped home at Uttoxeter so I can't see anything to touch him on that form. You've got a high class chaser there in my opinion."

Andy fairly basked in the praise. "Thanks Pete he's a really special horse, is he still favourite?"

"I expect you had a nice bet before the Uttoxeter race." Pete tapped the side of his nose. "He was eleven to ten on when I last looked. You should be able to see the bookies' boards down in the ring if you use your binoculars." He pointed with his head toward the balcony.

"So you think he'll win?" Miriam smiled at the thought of the horse winning and upsetting Andy's plans.

"Well there's no such thing as, you know, a sure thing in racing but as I said, on the form of his last race he should."

"What about the exchanges?" Andy fiddled with the stem of his glass and tried to sound casual.

"Not my department. You need that girl from the racing channel with her infernal computer thing; she'd tell you." He moved toward the door. "Good luck, have a great day and perhaps we'll talk again in the winner's enclosure." With that he was gone to dance the same tune for some other group of corporately entertained punters.

In twos and threes Andy's guests were looking at the race cards or the racing papers comparing notes and discussing Pete McIlroy's tips. The cacophony of sound multiplied by the general buzz from the race course as the crowds filtered in.

The happy mood was broken by the sound of a spoon banging on the table. "Ladies and gentlemen if you would like to take your seats lunch is ready to be served." The Banqueting Manager nodded and the waitresses bustled in with baskets of bread rolls and stood ready to start serving as people sorted themselves out at the table.

"Look for your place names everybody." Andy raised his voice above the chatter. "When you've picked out a horse that you would like to back let Debbie know and she'll put your bet on at the Tote. First race in 45 minutes."

Miriam scanned the place names anxiously. She just knew that Andy would have made sure she was next to him. Yes there it was. Her name next to his with the Swedish marketing director Lennart on her other side. She looked round for her husband and caught his eye as he stood behind his chair on the opposite side of the table. He gave her a reassuring smile before turning back to his conversation with his lunch partner Annie Nicol.

Once the ladies were seated, the men sat down and the level of noise increased as the first course was served and conversations started or resumed.

Why have you been avoiding me?" Andy leaned toward Miriam. "I hope you placed the bets as I said."

"Don't be silly." She gave a small laugh. "I've been busy that's all and yes I managed to get a couple or so bets on."

"How much did you get on?" His voice was tense and he fought hard to stop from clutching her arm.

"Can we all go into the parade ring, Andy?" Vincent's voice came from across the table anxious to relieve any pressure that his wife might be feeling from Andy's close attention.

"Yes, I expect so. When that damn trainer of mine gets here I'll make sure he fixes it." Anxious to get the answer to his question he turned back to Miriam.

But Miriam, thankful of her husband's interruption had seized the opportunity to speak to Lennart on her other side. "Isn't this exciting? I mean going into the parade ring and everything." God I must sound banal she thought to herself. "Oh I'm sorry. You do speak English?"

Lennart put down his knife and fork. "As the international business language you bet I do." His voice had an American twang. "First time for me – horse racing in England. How about you?"

"I've been before." She felt herself blush remembering Uttoxeter. "Are you going to back Andy's horse?"

Hearing his name gave Andy the chance to join the conversation. "I should jolly well hope so. Chance to cover the cost of your hotel, Lennart."

"But not the cost of my wife's little shopping trip." Lennart chuckled looking across the table at his wife. "Can't resist Bond Street isn't that right, Ulla?"

Andy leaned close to Miriam. "How much did you get on?" His voiced hissed between clenched teeth.

"Just over a hundred thousand." Afraid that her face would give her away she glanced quickly toward Lennart. "I just love shopping on Bond Street and wandering up and down those lovely arcades."

"Did I hear the word shopping?" Annie called down the table her Swedish accent making it sound like chopping. "Who's going chopping?"

The banter continued around the table. Andy sat with his fists clenched as he silently wondered at what odds the money had been wagered. If the average odds of the bets were even money the return would pay off his bank overdraft. And there would be enough over to get Don bloody Markham off his back. A smile played round the edges of his mouth at the thought of Don's face when the money he had spent was put back into the business.

"I said Adrian Markham's here." Debbie was leaning one hand on the back of his chair. "Are you alright?"

"Yes of course I'm alright." So focused were his thoughts on the outcome of the race that he hadn't heard her the first time. Andy pushed back his chair and strode round the table to the door where Adrian was standing. Grabbing him by the arm and bundling him outside before anyone could speak he was anxious to know that everything was going to plan.

"Where have you been?" He hissed. "You weren't in the owners and trainers earlier, I looked."

"I do have other runners today and owners that need looking after." Adrian shrugged out of Andy's grip. "Any way I said I'd come to the box. What's the matter you look worried?"

Having fought his frustration all morning he couldn't help but let rip. "Of course I'm fucking worried." He snarled. "I won't stop worrying until the bloody race is over and the horse has lost. I'll be smiling then and counting the cash all the way to the bank."

"I still don't like this you know." Adrian looked up and down the corridor. "If we get caught..."

"There's nothing to catch us at, besides which you'll do nicely out it." Andy pushed open the door and ushered Adrian forward. "Now come in, have some lunch and meet my guests."

He led Adrian round to an empty seat at the foot of the table. "Meet Adrian everybody he trains Alternative Ways. Get your race cards out and he'll tip you a few winners."

Making his way back to his own place at the table Andy sat down and pushed away his half-eaten plate of wild mushroom risotto. There was an unfamiliar knot of tension that had settled in his stomach. He'd never felt so tense before. He forced himself to smile as Ulla called across the table.

"Adrian says we can go into the parade ring before the start of the race. Are we going to be on television?" Her voice was full of excitement.

"The whole race will be on television and the cameras are bound to pick you out." Andy nodded, his eyes drawn toward the expanse of cleavage that Ulla was displaying. "Who could resist your charms?"

The plates were cleared and the next course was served. Debbie had been round and written down the horses that each of the guests wanted to back in the first two races.

"I'm going to put these bets on with the tote" she bent down and spoke into Andy's ear "but I'm going to need some money unless you want me to ask the guest to pay for their bets."

"No, no don't do that." He leaned back in his chair and pushed his hand into his pocket. "Here's a hundred." Counting out five twenty pound notes he passed them over his shoulder. "And put this hundred on Boy Wonder in the first, there's a good girl." Another five twenty pound notes were counted from the bundle.

A man from the caterers fiddled with the television set that was fixed to an extending arm bolted on the wall of the box. The voice of the race course commentator filled the room and a picture of the parade ring flashed onto the screen.

"Here we go - runners for the first race." Lennart's voice was raised to be heard above the sound of the commentator. All eyes focused on the screen as the jockeys mounted their horses and were led down the walkway and released onto the course.

"I'm going out onto the balcony to watch this." Vincent stood up. "Come on Miriam." He pulled back the sliding door to the balcony and waited as she pushed back her chair and made her way round the table.

Out on the balcony he put his arm round her and gave her a hug. "Not giving you a hard time is he?"

She shook her head. "No. He asked how much money I'd managed to bet. I told him just over a hundred thousand pounds."

"Good. That should keep him on edge. Did you see him dishing out the lolly – my lolly I hasten to add?" The loudspeakers in the stands cut through their conversation 'Coming into line for our first race – and they're off.'

The door opened behind them and Andy and Lennart came out. "Did you back anything Vincent?" Andy put his hand on Vincent's shoulder. "I had a few bob on Boy Wonder."

"Only a fiver on the favourite." The thunder of the racing horse as they swept past and the roar of the crowd almost drowned out his words.

"Golly its cold out here." Miriam shivered. "I think I'll go in and watch it on the TV."

Left alone the three men stood in silence and watched the horses on the far side of the course.

Andy had his binoculars up to his eyes. "Boy Wonder's just moving up to challenge your horse for the lead, Vincent." He turned and smiled. "Twenty quid says I'll beat you."

Before Vincent could reply a groan went up from the crowd in the grandstand below them. "Boy Wonder's gone at the sixth," the commentator's voice boomed above the noise of the crowd, "horse and jockey both on their feet."

"Twenty quid wasn't it?" Vincent's smile beamed across his face. "Oh dear and you backed it as well."

Pulling a note from his pocket Andy thrust it into Vincent's outstretched hand. "Double or quits on the next." He sneered, making it a challenge not a question although inside the anxiety and doubt were gnawing at him. Was this an omen? Would his luck run out?

Watching the favourite win comfortably before replying Vincent could feel the tension emanating from Andy. "Yes, why not." He laughed. "A nice win on the Tote, your twenty quid. I'll not be using any of my money. What's your fancy?" He just glimpsed the look of pure malice as Andy turned away and opened the door from the balcony.

"The champion jockey's chosen to ride Paper Clip rather than his stable's horse so I'll go for that." He stepped into the box leaving the others to follow.

Vincent ushered Lennart through the door then slid it closed against the chill of the October afternoon. "Have you picked up my winnings yet Debbie?" He called as he sat down at the table and picked up the race card. "I need to pick another winner to teach your boss that the last one wasn't just a fluke."

Debbie glanced at Andy as he tipped champagne into his glass and swallowed it in a couple of gulps. "Thirty two pounds and…" She counted the money onto the table. "Seventeen pence. Well done,

Mr Floyd. I'll follow your tip next time." She smiled at Andy who glared back at her.

"Put this on Paper Clip." He pulled ten notes from the bundle. "This bottle's empty." Nodding at the waiter hovering near the bar. "Tell them they need to stay on top if they think they're getting a tip from me."

"My, my we are getting tetchy." Suzanne slid into the seat next to him. "Only one more race then your precious horse will be able to do its stuff and you can relax."

"Talking of which." Adrian stood up. "I have to go but I'll see you all in the parade ring. You need to be there ten minutes before the off."

There was the slightest hint of a slur in Andy's voice. "Let's hope everything goes to plan." He tapped the side of his nose.

Nodding to the rest of the guests Adrian walked out of the box to head toward the race course stables where Alternative Ways was waiting.

"Chosen your horse yet Floyd?" Andy's voice was harsh. "After all you're the expert as you've had one winner."

"As a matter of fact I have. He pointed to the racing paper. "Seems that a little bird on the gallops has been watching Silk Screen, the bottom weight and likes the look of it. So Debbie, could you put me twenty pounds to win, please?"

The room buzzed as everyone discussed the merits of the horses in the next. All that is except Andy who was doing his best to empty the bottle that had been put down in front of him. Images of watchers on the gallops disturbed him. His jaw clenched as he tried to put any ideas from his mind that his scheme to make money could be jeopardised. At the start of the race they all crowded onto the balcony leaving Andy alone with his thoughts and fears.

The sliding of the door and excited babble as they came back in laughing and reaching for their champagne glasses startled him from his almost trance like state.

"Good old Vincent had twenty quid on the winner at odds of six to one – isn't that great?" Lennart slapped him on the back. "This is really good." He pulled his wife close to him. "Ulla picked the same horse but only put two pounds on. Still a win is a win. What do you say Andy?"

"He gets another forty quid from me that's what I say." With ill grace he flung forty ponds on the table. "Get your coats on we need to be going down to the ring."

Pocketing the money Vincent smirked with self-satisfaction. "Hope you have better luck with your horse. Be a shame if he lost. I expect you've had a good bet on him?"

Ignoring him Andy slipped his arms into the overcoat being offered by one of the staff. He stood waiting until they were all suitably wrapped up against the cold and then led the way from the box to the lift. As the doors slid open at the ground floor they emerged out into the crowds thronging and bustling in their attempts to get to the parade ring to see the horses.

Chapter 22

The steward guarding the entrance checked their badges carefully before allowing them into the parade ring. The rails that separated the walkway inside the ring and the path outside was lined five deep with spectators. Each one seemingly anxious to check out their fancy before plunging hard earned money on a bet with the bookmakers or the Tote.

In the centre of the ring, on the oval of bright green turf, stood small groups of owners and friends. Some laughing and talking nervously some excitedly, as they waited for their horses to enter. This was not the summer dress brigade of Royal Ascot but the tweed skirt, leather boots and fur hat stalwarts of National Hunt racing.

As they came into the parade ring the horses were led round; coloured rugs strapped across their backs with the trainer's initials woven into one corner. The handlers leading the horses were well wrapped against the cold. Their jackets sported the emblem and name of the yard's sponsor.

"What are those numbers on the arms of the people with the horses?" Helena Carlson looked quizzically at Andy.

"That's the horse's number on the race card." Andy was pleased to show off and take the opportunity to move closer to Helena. He could smell her musky perfume as he leant against her and opened his race card. Funny how his tension slipped away as he breathed in that earthy smell. "Here you are." He looked up as a horse jigged its way past them. "Number six on his arm and," pointing to the race card, "Never Last. Hmm I don't think I'd name one of my horses that."

"Look." Helena pulled away and pointed to the opening in the parade ring where the horses entered. "I recognise the Clewer Alternatives logo on that man's jacket. That must be your horse."

Squinting into the October sunshine Andy recognised Cowboy leading the horse.

"Here he comes, everybody." The tension was back immediately as he watched Alternative Ways stride majestically around the walkway, hindquarters gleaming the colour of burnished copper and looking every inch the favourite.

Adrian Fordham followed the horse into the parade ring and spotting his owner marched purposefully toward Andy and his entourage.

"Afternoon everybody." He lifted his brown trilby and nodded his head toward the ladies. "Hope you've all placed your bets as there won't be much time after the horses have left the ring."

"Miriam's put my money on, haven't you darling? Vincent smiled at his wife. "My God Adrian, these horses look fit."

"A lot of time, effort and hard work goes into getting them here, at their peak, on the day." He glanced at Andy who stood shoulders hunched against the bitter wind that swirled round the ring. "Owners wouldn't thank you if not. That right Andy?"

"Too true now what orders will you be giving to Wayne?" The jockeys had come from the weighing room and into the parade ring and were seeking out the owners and their connections. He waved his arm and Wayne veered toward them.

They all grouped round Adrian as he introduced Wayne Packard the stable jockey. Wayne touched his whip to his cap and shook hands with each of them in turn then waited for his riding instructions.

"Keep him covered up on the first circuit." Adrian kept his voice low and they all strained to listen. "If he's still on the bridle three out make your move from there. Up the hill to the line won't be a worry but I don't won't you to be hard on him." He turned to Andy. "No sense in punishing the horse if he hasn't got the stamina to last out."

Andy's face was pale and there was a slight tic pulsing near his right eye. "No, quite right. Just do your best Wayne, good luck."

The bell rang and the handlers turned the horses off the tarmac walkway and onto the grass. "I'll give Wayne a leg up and join you in the box." Adrian called over his shoulder as he and Wayne started to thread their way through the melee of people and horses.

With Andy leading they pushed and barged their way through the crowds. A cacophony of sound made it virtually impossible to speak with each other until they reached the sanctuary of their private box.

"Out onto the balcony and we can see the horses go down to the start. They'll parade in front of the stands." Andy ushered everyone out through the sliding doors talking as he did so to hide the feeling of anxiety that sat like a ball of lead in the pit of his stomach.

"The horses are leaving the paddock" the voice of the racecourse commentator boomed from above them "number nine Morning Glory has won the prize for the best turned out horse." There was a pause before he continued. "They're coming out now led by Blue Jeans, followed by Calculator." Andy wasn't listening as the commentator's voice droned on reciting the names of each horse as they paraded in front of the huge crowd in the stands. He raised his binoculars and focused on Alternative Ways as the horse was led out onto the track. Wayne perched on top looking cool and confident as the horse jinked from side to side, tossing his head and eying the waving arms of the race goers that packed the rails beside the course.

Reaching the end of the stands the horses were turned by their handlers who slipped the leading reins allowing their charges to surge away down the course toward the start of the two mile steeplechase.

Andy's knuckles whitened as he gripped the binoculars. He turned his body so as to follow the horse's progress down the course. A breathless Adrian eased himself onto the balcony and stood behind him.

"He's moving well." Adrian murmured into Andy's ear. "He's still favourite but only just. There's a lot of money coming for the Irish horse Just a Dream."

"Huh." Andy grunted concentrating his binoculars on the group of horses arriving down at the start watching as last minute adjustments were made to the girths that held the saddle in place.

As they walked round in a circle the starter climbed up onto his rostrum. Pausing to check on the line of horses he raised a flag above his head. The jockeys turned their horses, jostling for position, to face the starting line.

"We have a new favourite" the commentator advised the crowd "Just a Dream is now even money with Alternative Ways at six to four against. They're under starter's orders … and they're off."

"Is that good six to four against?" Ulla grabbed hold of Andy's arm, causing the binoculars to shake.

"Look what you're doing." He snapped at her pulling his arm free. "Can't you see I'm trying to watch the bloody race" Binoculars back to eyes he was oblivious to the stares of his guests at his outburst.

"Steady on old boy." George Nicol put a reassuring hand on Ulla's shoulder. "I know it's a big race and all but no need for that. Yes my dear, you see you put four pounds on the horse to win and get six pounds back."

"Oh so I win two pounds." Ulla frowned in disappointment. "That doesn't seem very good.

"No, no you also get your four pounds back so you win six." George smiled. "150 percent return not bad eh?"

Andy kept his binoculars firmly gripped to his eyes, taking no part in the conversation as he followed the horses up the straight and away round the turn at the top of the hill.

"Sorry everyone." He lowered the binoculars and gave them a quick lop sided grin. "This race means a lot to me." He resumed his avid watch on the race.

"There's a faller at the water jump," the commentator's voice brought the race back in focus, "Morning Glory's gone at that one and badly hampered Alternative Ways."

A groan went up from the gathering on the balcony, only Andy remained silent as the leaders took the next, the open ditch.

"Wayne's giving him a breather and a chance to gather himself as they run downhill." Adrian had his own binoculars trained on the race and didn't take his eyes of the horse as he delivered his own private commentary. "Come on now Wayne move a bit closer before the bottom of the hill."

They took the second open ditch and rounded the turn three fences from home. Alternative Ways was in sixth place almost twelve lengths behind the leading horses when Wayne let the reins out a notch and began to make up ground.

"The favourite seems to be going well." Adrian had focused on Just a Dream who raced in second place two lengths behind the leader. "But our boy's making ground now."

Alternative Ways had drawn level with Blue Jeans at the third fence from home but had out jumped him to land a length ahead in fifth place. He was full of running and gaining ground on the horses in front.

"Just a Dream's hit the front with two fences to jump" the commentator boomed, "and Alternative Ways is trying hard to get on terms and has moved into third."

Andy gritted his teeth as he willed his horse to run out of stamina. Alternative Ways flew the second last with a leap that brought cheers from the crowd who were sensing that the favourite might not get things all his own way.

As they rounded the turn to head up the hill to the final fence and the run in to the winning post there were three horses almost in a line. "Just a Dream is in front by half a length from Calculator and Alternative Ways who race together" an excited commentator shouted "it's going to be down to who can jump the last fence the better."

"Come on, come on." Andy hadn't realised he'd shouted out aloud as he willed the favourite on to win. His hands gripped the binoculars so hard that his knuckles hurt.

The leading horse jumped the last and set sail for the winning post. Calculator and Alternative Ways landed together. Wayne asked his horse for one final effort and they surged up the hill after the leader. Calculator was left struggling in third place.

Just a Dream's tiring." Adrian shouted to anyone who was listening. "Come on AW show them what you're made of." The gap between the two horses was diminishing with every stride. Each horse and jockey strained to reach the winning line first. With fifty yards to go there was less than half a length between them. Wayne was pumping his arms in rhythm with the horse's gallop. Just a Dream was under the whip and not finding anymore.

They flashed over the line seemingly locked together. "Who won, who won?" Suzanne was punching Andy's arm with frustration. "Did we win?"

Andy lowered his binoculars and turned with a glazed look in his eyes. "God knows, I don't." His shoulders sagged and he thrust his hands deep into his coat pockets so that no one could see them shaking.

Adrian rushed from the box to check on the horse. "Photograph, photograph," called the loudspeaker, "the result has gone to a photograph."

"Come on Andy let's go down to the winner's enclosure." Lennart put an arm across his shoulders and guided him towards the door. "You might've won." The others crowded through the doorway and into the corridor all talking at the same time.

"I'm sure you've won." Said Ulla. "From where I was it looked like Just a Dream had his nose in front," argued George Nicol. Marcus Carlson nodded his agreement. "Yes I think so too."

As they waited for the lift Andy shook his head. "After everything it's all down to a photograph." The excited discussion continued around him as they squeezed themselves into the lift the moment doors opened.

Once down stairs they made their way to the enclosure in front of the weighing room. A steward ushered the crowd back so that they could walk into the enclosure where the horses were due to arrive at any moment judging by the cheers of the crowd that lined the walkway from the course.

Blue Jeans was led into the spot for the fourth home. Alternative Ways was the next to enter led by Cowboy with Adrian following behind. Cowboy walked the horse round in a tight circle, not going into the winner or runner up spots as they waited for the result of the photograph.

"What the bloody hell are they doing?" The tic beside Andy's eye had started up again. "Can't you find out Adrian instead of just bloody well-?"

An announcement drowned out the rest of his sentence. "Here is the result of the photograph. First number six - Alternative Ways. Second number four - Just a Dream. Third number eight - Calculator and fourth number twelve - Blue Jeans."

Andy could feel the energy drain from his body as he stood, numb and withdrawn. Around him his guests were cheering as Cowboy led the horse into the winner's enclosure.

A television interviewer accompanied by a cameraman pushed through the happy group. "Mr Clewer, could we have you by the horse please?"

As if in a trance Andy felt himself being pushed forward. His hand was shaken half a dozen times as he received congratulations from race course officials and the owners of the runner up. He moved with Adrian to stand next to Alternative Ways.

The horse's flanks were still heaving from the effort of the race and were giving off clouds of steam which hung in the cold air. He had a sheet draped over his back emblazoned with the alphabet logo of the XYZ Engineering Group, sponsors of the race. Wayne Packard had his arm round the horse's neck grinning at anyone who looked at him.

The words of the interviewer cut through Andy's state of limbo. "Congratulations Mr Clewer a hard fought race did you think you'd win?" A light on the camera glowed red and a microphone was thrust in front of his chest.

Gathering himself he struggled to respond. "He's a tough horse." He managed to say gulping and coughing in an attempt to hide his dazed feelings. "I'm very pleased for Adrian Fordham and my jockey Wayne Packard."

The interviewer turned his attention to Adrian pressing him to comment on the plans for the horse's future. "Will he go for the Champion Chase at next year's Cheltenham Festival?"

"It's too soon to say. We'll get the horse home make sure he's come out of the race OK and take it from there." Adrian patted the horse's neck.

"Horses away please, horses away." The clerk of the course called above the clamour of proud connections.

Cowboy turned the horse and walked him from the ring toward the stables. The Managing Director of the sponsors was heading for the podium set up at the centre of the winner's enclosure where a table was laden with silverware. Taking pride of place was a 12 inch diameter silver salver.

The television screens around the course, in betting shops and in homes across the nation showed Andy and Suzanne receiving the gleaming salver. Suzanne also got a bouquet and a kiss on the cheek from the sponsor. Adrian received a silver tankard and a jubilant Wayne a magnum of champagne and a small silver shield.

The Clewer party stood and cheered as they too soaked up the limelight. Reporters and cameramen were everywhere. Pete McIlroy was his usual ebullient self, interviewing Miriam and Anne Carlson, the two most attractive of the women in the party. He got them to confirm that he had predicted the outcome of the race and urging television viewers to come racing and to follow the wisdom of his advice.

For Andy the rest of the afternoon passed in a haze of alcohol and worry over losing a hundred thousand pounds on the betting exchange. Only Adrian understood the morose expression on Andy's face and the lethargic way in which he joined in the celebrations moving like an automaton, a fixed smile on his lips.

Chapter 23

It was almost six o'clock more than two hours after the last race when they made their way back to the car park where their drivers were patiently waiting.

"Marvellous day, old man." Vincent slapped Andy on the back. "My turn to repay the hospitality. Lunch at our place eh, Miriam."

"Well, yes of course." She sounded flustered not sure if Vincent had had too much to drink. "When were you thinking of?"

"Tomorrow. What do you say?" He waved his arms in a sweeping motion. "All of you. George, Lennart, Marcus you're all invited."

"That's kind of you Vincent but we fly back to Sweden tomorrow. Perhaps another time would be good." Marcus pulled back his sleeve and glanced at his watch. "We must be going. We have dinner tonight with another of our suppliers. Our thanks Andy." He held out his hand as the others said their goodbyes. "We will show you racing Swedish style when next you come to visit."

"I'll go with you Mr Carlson, see you back safely to your hotel and pick up my car." Debbie walked over to the car which had brought the Swedes and spoke to the driver. She climbed into the front passenger seat leaving him to open the rear door and settle the others in the back. They waved as the car pulled away from the car park.

George Nicol made his excuses to Vincent. "Sorry to disappoint you but we are out to lunch tomorrow with our daughter and son in law. We're taking them to the Bridgedale. Some other time perhaps. Now where's that driver of mine."

There were more noisy goodbyes until only the four of them were left. Brian opened up the rear door and they climbed in. "Back to Richmond, Mr Clewer?"

"Yes, yes just get on and bloody drive." Andy slumped back in his seat the effort of trying to maintain a façade of exuberance at the horse's win was telling on him. He felt the others looking at him. "Sorry, Brian it's been a long day and I've probably had too much to drink."

"Well, well the great Andy Clewer apologising. We must get the horse to win more often." Suzanne switched on the light above her chair and opened the small beige leather shoulder bag that she had carried to the races. Pulling out a wad of crumpled banknotes she looked round the table at her fellow passengers. "I think I did quite well." She began to smooth the notes out onto the table in front of her.

"Let's see who's won the most." Miriam was anxious to do anything to take her mind off the brooding Andy. She pulled a purse from her coat pocket and switched on her light. "I don't seem to have as many notes as you, Suzanne."

"Ah but quite a few of yours are twenties, my dear. "Vincent laughed and leaned forward as he joined in the fun. "With the money I won from Andy and a couple of winning bets I was up over a hundred and fifty pounds. Unfortunately I backed losers in the last two races so I reckon I've won about a hundred. What about you Andy?"

For a brief moment the old arrogant Andy Clewer surfaced. "As you say, Vincent I lost a few quid to you and backed a couple of dodgy losers myself." He put both hands on the table and leaned forward into the lamplight and looked across at Vincent. "But I did back the horse before the race at odds of five to one." His face twisted into a malevolent grin. "So I think I beat you all. Ten thousand pounds at five to one makes me the winner with fifty thousand in the kitty." He looked round at each of them savouring the moment.

"Good for you. Just the one bet or have you covered yourself with even more glory." Vincent's voice was harsh with the thought that Andy might have won enough to repay the loan in full.

"What the hell's it got to do with you?" He slumped back into his seat. "I'm going to sleep." He closed his eyes and lay back motionless as the car sped on through the darkness of the motorway.

Andy's outburst had dampened the mood of the others and they too sought refuge from the strained atmosphere by cat napping for the rest of the journey.

"Just pulling into Old Deer Park Gardens Mr Floyd." Brian's voice caused a stretching and yawning from the dozing passengers as the pulled up in front of the Floyd's house.

"You've made good time Brian it's only just eight." Turning Vincent thrust out his hand. "No hard feelings on me winning our little bets."

"No. It's just that I don't like losing." Andy took his hand. "Are you sure about lunch tomorrow?"

"Well actually, Vincent." Miriam spoke hesitantly. "I'm not sure that we've got anything in for lunch tomorrow. Why not make it another day?"

"Yes of course why not Tuesday. Make it a late celebration of your win." Brian had opened the door and Vincent got out followed by Miriam. Putting his head back inside he smiled at Suzanne. "Our place, say about one o'clock, would that suit?"

"That would be lovely Vincent dear." She leaned forward to give him a kiss on the cheek. "We'll see you then."

The Floyds stood on the doorstep and waved as Brian drove off. With a sigh Vincent took out his keys and unlocked the door.

"Well I'm glad that's over." He stood back as he opened the door for Miriam turning on the lights as he followed her in. "Can't understand why the bloody man's so miserable." Shutting the front door he shrugged out of his coat and threw it over the banisters.

"I'm going upstairs to change. Do you want anything to eat?" Miriam slipped off the gloves she was wearing and started up the stairs. "What about cheese and biscuits?"

"M'mm, yes why not." Vincent wandered through to the kitchen. There was just over half a bottle of red wine on the worktop with a screw cap that had kept it fresh. He took two glasses from the cupboard and poured himself out a drink.

Miriam swept into the kitchen and pulled the fridge open. "You look thoughtful. Ah, there's some brie and a piece of that mature cheddar that you like."

"It worries me that Clewer wasn't more, what's the word, you know more elated about his win. After all he thinks you put a hundred thousand pounds in bets on for him so he must reckon he's got a fair wedge of money coming to him."

"I'll have a glass of that red, please darling and get two plates out will you." She busied herself unwrapping the cheese and getting biscuits out of the larder. "I was supposed to back his horse to lose." She called over her shoulder. "Didn't I tell you that?"

"You were supposed to do what?" Plates clattered and Vincent raised his voice in surprise. "The horse was practically red hot favourite right up to the off. Why on earth would he back it to lose, it just doesn't make sense?"

"Come and sit down." She brought the cheese and the tin of biscuits over and put them on the table. "I don't know why, when I asked him he got abusive and told me just to get on and do it. Now what are you thinking about?"

"He must have had a damn good reason for wagering that amount of money on the horse to lose. He was up to something. When we agreed the loan he couldn't wait to get out of the office with the bankers draft."

Miriam couldn't stop herself from blushing. "He was meeting me. I'm sorry darling, but he wanted me to put the money in my account." She pulled out a chair and sat at the table. "He rang me and we arranged to meet in Kingston."

"And then he wanted you to put the bet on." Vincent knelt down beside her and smiled. "We can't change what happened, my dearest and until we've sorted him out there's going to be times when we both feel awkward. But it'll be OK I promise you." She leant forward and kissed him gently.

"Come and get this cheese and biscuits." She pulled away from him. "What's this lunch all about on Tuesday?"

"It's come-uppance time for Mr Andy Clewer and what you've just told me makes it even better." He sat down beside her and helped himself to a chunk of cheddar. "Pass the biscuits will you?"

Selecting two biscuits she pushed the tin toward him. "So what does that mean?"

"My darling, its better that you don't know. If you should speak to him or bump into him you won't be able to give anything away if you don't know anything, will you?" He cut a piece off the cheddar on his plate, balanced it on a biscuit and took a bite. "This cheddar nearly bites you back it's so strong."

"I'd better start thinking about what we're going to eat on Tuesday." Miriam took a sip of wine. "Do you want a buffet or a proper sit down meal?"

"Don't you worry. I'll organise the caterers from the office to come in and do us something. Better still I'll get them to give you a ring on Monday morning and you can sort it out with them. Don Markham will be joining us as well as the Clewers. Now come on and eat up. I recorded that celebrity dancing programme that you like. We can watch that before we go to bed."

***

Suzanne and Andy rode home in silence. Brian waited to watch him open up the front door before driving away. Andy went straight through to the cocktail cabinet and poured himself half a tumbler of malt whisky.

"Don't you think you've had enough to drink?" Suzanne shrugged out of her coat and draped it over the back of the sofa.

"You don't know what I've had enough of." He took a deep gulp of his drink and spluttered as it went down the wrong way. "Look what you've bloody well made me do now." He wiped his mouth with the back of his hand. "Why don't you go to bed or something? Just leave me alone." He slumped down on the sofa and stared morosely at the floor.

"The mood you're in it'll be a pleasure. You can sleep in the spare room again tonight and see if that improves your mood." Picking up her coat Suzanne went out closing the door behind her. She went through to the kitchen and put some milk on to heat up. There was a novel she'd just started and having made herself a mug of drinking chocolate she put out the lights and climbed the stairs.

She took off her clothes and slipped on her robe. Pulling back the bedclothes she sat up in bed and started reading her book. About half an hour later she could hear Andy coming up the stairs. She waited fully expecting him to walk into the bedroom. He mumbled something and then she heard the door to the guest bedroom bang shut.

Breathing a sigh of relief she put her book down. He was definitely acting strangely. After the horse winning and the bet he'd boasted about she thought he would have been his usual larger than life self. She climbed out of bed and went to her dressing table. She reached for the cotton wool and using it gently massaged cleansing milk onto her face to get rid of her make up. Going through to the en-suite she rinsed her face in warm water and cleaned and flossed her teeth before getting back into bed.

It had been a long day. With all the excitement and tension, the champagne and the wine she felt quite tired. 'Lunch on Tuesday should be fun' she thought to herself as she put the light off and settled down.

Chapter 24

The bedroom door creaked open as Miriam pushed it with her hip manoeuvring a laden tray through the opening. Vincent yawned and stretched before turning his head and peering with bleary eyes at his wife.

"I thought you might like breakfast in bed this morning." She put the tray onto the dressing table. "Come on sit up. I'll get your dressing gown."

"My, my but you're spoiling me." Sitting up Vincent leaned forward and Miriam put the dressing gown round his shoulders. "Good Lord is that the time." He stared at the clock. A quarter past nine. Good job I cancelled my golf today." He pushed his arms into the sleeves and leaned back against the pillows.

"Pull back those bed clothes." Miriam balanced the tray as she slipped back into bed. "There, croissants, orange juice and marmalade. That should get the day off to a good start."

"All the better for you joining me." He gently rubbed her arm. "What shall we do today?"

"How about a walk down by the river? It looks like being another nice day and we could have some lunch in that pub by Hampton Court." Miriam broke off a piece of croissant and spread it with marmalade.

"Yes why not." Vincent picked up his coffee cup and took a sip. "I've got to ring Don Markham today."

"Don, whatever for?"

"To get things set up for Tuesday." Vincent's mouth twitched into a mischievous grin. "He's part of the plot and will be with us for the lunch, not that Clewer will know until he gets here."

"Are you sure about all this? Anxiety showed in Miriam's voice. "I mean it's not illegal or anything, what you and Don have planned?"

"Let's just say its sharp practice." Vincent stuffed the last of the croissants into his mouth. "No more than Clewer would do if the boot was on the other foot so to speak."

***

In spite of an afternoon of drinking and the couple of stiff malt whiskies before bed, Andy had spent most of the previous night tossing and turning. Sleep had eluded him as he grappled with the thought of losing a hundred thousand pounds, not to mention money he had spent on the cars, the box at the races and his losing wagers that in effect, he didn't really have. The prize money from the horse winning today would go straight to the Company as Andy was only owner in name the horses being bought by the Company so he couldn't count on that. Convinced that he would win sufficient money to end all his worries he was finding it hard to cope with the sense of utter desolation that overwhelmed him. An exhausted sleep had finally come in the early hours of the morning.

"You're up at last." Suzanne, seated at the table in her dressing gown, was drinking coffee as Andy, showered and shaved, came into the kitchen. "You were in a grotty mood yesterday."

"For Christ's sake don't start." He opened the fridge and stared inside. "Where's the bloody orange juice?"

"It's here on the table. Get yourself a glass. What are you doing today?" Suzanne topped up her coffee cup.

Andy glanced at the kitchen clock. "I thought I'd take a run over to the stables – see how the horse is after the race. I'll have lunch with Adrian." He sorted through the Sunday papers until he found the sports section.

"Good, with this bright morning sunlight I'm going to start on a painting in the workshop." Suzanne finished her coffee and carefully patted her lips on a pale blue napkin. "Roast lamb for dinner tonight. Could you make sure you're back by six thirty." With his head buried in the paper she took Andy's grunt as confirmation.

***

The yard was deserted when Andy pulled in. Heads appeared and looked out over stable doors with ears flicking at the sound of his car but there were no obvious signs of human presence.

Getting out he walked past the office and under an archway that led to a flag stoned courtyard. At the rear was the door to Adrian's bachelor flat built above old store rooms. Banging on the door Andy called out. Moments later a window above his head opened and Adrian looked out.

"Oh, it's you. I'll be down in a minute." Footsteps sounded on wooden stairs and a moment later the door was flung back to reveal a dishevelled Adrian Fordham. "We celebrated a bit last night." He stifled a yawn. "I was just catching a quick nap after feeding the horses. Come to see your boy have you.?"

"Yeah and to see what went wrong with our bloody plan. Christ you can't begin to know what deep shit I'm in. I'd banked on the horse losing, what went wrong for crying out loud?"

Shutting the door Adrian started across the courtyard. "The horse just doesn't know when to lie down and get beaten. He wasn't as fit as he should have been but he still battled on and won." He suddenly stopped walking and turned to Andy. "That horse is a bloody marvel. The way he jumps, his stamina and will to win could make him the next Arkle. I'm convinced there's plenty more good races to be won."

"Well there may not be any more races if I can't sort out the mess I'm in. It's absolute hell smiling and pretending how great it is that the horse won." As if on cue Alternative Ways looked out of his stable and whinnied.

They stood looking at the horse. "He's come out of it well." Adrian rubbed the soft velvet of the horse's nose. "He's a bit stiff but no more than I'd expect after a hard race. I'm thinking of entering him into the King George at Kempton on Boxing Day." He turned to look at Andy. "What do you think?"

"The King George, I like the sound of that. The prizes are usually presented by Royalty." Andy gazed across the yard a faraway look in his eye. "That would put me into a different league altogether." His mind was working overtime. He could see himself being invited to Royal Garden Parties, photographed with the Queen maybe. "Yes, let's aim for that." He clapped Adrian on the shoulder. "Gives us something to look forward to."

They walked down the lane to the village for lunch at the pub and for the next two hours sat over beer and sandwiches making plans for Alternative Ways. "I've got to get back and check on the horses. Adrian drained his glass and stood up.

Back in the yard the two men shook hands. There was almost a spring in Andy's step as he headed back to his car. Things weren't that bad. There was still a hell of a lot of money in Miriam's bank account and more than three months to the end of the company's financial year before the money need be paid back.

Back at home Suzanne was standing at the stove basting the potatoes round the meat when he walked in. She noted with surprise that he was whistling.

Chapter 25

"Miriam, at bloody last. Has he gone to work, can you talk?" Andy used the car phone as he drove into the office the Monday morning after the race. He didn't give her the chance to reply so eager was he to get his hands on some more money. "Meet me in that Italian place in Kingston. We need to get some cash from the bank."

His face darkened as he listened. "Tell him you've got a headache or something. Good God it's only a trip to the Tate you could go another day." Bloody Vincent wanting to go to art galleries.

"Well if you won't wriggle out of it make sure you get another ten thousand pounds for me." He frowned. "We're seeing you for lunch tomorrow you can slip the money to me then." His voice softened. "Are you sure you can't get away, I've missed you. It's been a while since we made love."

Miriam struggled to keep her voice normal. "I know but maybe once this lunch thing is out of the way. Look I've got to go Vincent's sent a car for me. I'll see you tomorrow."

"Don't forget ..." Andy spoke to a phone that had gone dead. "Bloody woman she'd better bring the money."

He arrived at the office to be greeted by Debbie with a full agenda for the day. The time was soon swallowed up with meetings, a lunch with the company's auditors and a presentation by the product development team. He had to endure the congratulations on the horse's win reminding him once again of how much money he had lost.

At the end of the day he wasn't ready to go home to Suzanne. For some reason Miriam was playing hard to get so he turned his attentions on Debbie when she called out to him that she was going.

"Just hang on a minute will you." He called back to her. "Come in here for a moment." He stood up from his desk and walked toward the door as she came in. "You haven't got to rush off straight away, have you?" He closed the door behind her and she turned to face him.

"Did you enjoy your day at the races?" He caught hold of her hand. "Perhaps you could show me how grateful you are."

Pulling her hand away from his she took a step backwards. "I'm sorry Andy, it won't work anymore. You've just been using me to satisfy yourself when you couldn't have one of your lady friends."

"But that's not true Debbie, I really care for you." He tried to reach for her hand but she moved further away.

"The other week you couldn't wait to get out of here after your meeting with Vincent Floyd. When you came in that morning you said we could meet later. I heard you on the phone arranging to meet someone." She fought back the tears and struggled to keep her voice level. "You'd forgotten all about me. Well you're not going to use me anymore. Let me out please, I want to go home."

"Well go on then you silly bitch." He strode over to the door and flung it open. "Off you go." Debbie almost ran from the room.

***

The next morning Andy was in the office before eight o'clock. He had arranged that Suzanne would make her own way to the Floyd's for lunch and he wanted to placate Debbie in case she knew more than she'd let on yesterday. The last thing he wanted was his secretary blabbing all over the place.

There was no sign of her by nine o'clock and he began to worry that she might be up to something. He heard the door to her office open and sprang up from his desk and peered round the door. It wasn't Debbie; it was only the post being delivered.

With no secretary he thought he might as well open the post himself. There was an envelope marked 'Personal – Addressee Eyes Only'. He ripped it open and read Debbie's letter of resignation.

"Oh bloody great." He shouted throwing the letter down onto the desk. "As if I haven't got enough worries." He marched back to his desk and picked up the phone. Punching out the number for Don's extension he drummed his fingers on the desk as he waited while the phone rang. After four rings it cut into voicemail. He slammed the receiver back onto the cradle and stared at the rest of his unopened post.

"Great day this is going to be." He idly sifted through the envelopes without much interest until he saw one bearing the franked logo of his bank. "May as well get all the bad news out of the way." Using a letter opener he slit the envelope and pulled out a single page. It was a Company bank statement showing that twenty five thousand pounds had been deposited courtesy of a transfer from Weatherbys Bank.

"Oh damn and blast." He had completely forgotten that he'd made an arrangement for any excess cash in the Weatherbys' account to be automatically transferred to the Company bank account. They administered all horse racing activities in the country and the prize money from the XYZ Handicap had been transferred across the moment it had been paid in.

It would take him about half an hour to reach the Floyd's house at this time of the day. He checked his watch. Eleven thirty another hour to kill. He picked up the paper and moved round to sit on the sofa. He managed to pass forty minutes reading the paper and then got up, checked he had his car keys and wandered out of the office. Minutes later he was behind the wheel of the Aston Martin and heading for Richmond.

Vincent Floyd opened the door to him. "Come in, everybody's here. Drink before lunch?"

"I'll have a beer if you've got one." He moved through to the lounge looking round for Miriam. Instead he saw Don Markham. "Don, what the hell are you doing here?"

"Just joining in the celebrations." Don raised his glass toward Andy. "Couldn't miss out on your big day now could I?"

"Thanks." Andy took the glass of beer that Vincent offered him. "Where are the girls?"

"Oh they're around somewhere." Vincent clicked his fingers. "Of course I nearly forgot. You're expecting Miriam to have something for you aren't you?"

"What do you mean?" Andy took a quick gulp of his beer. "I just wondered where they were that's all."

"A little matter of ten thousand pounds, isn't that right, darling?" He turned as Suzanne and Miriam came into the room.

Miriam put her arm round her husband's waist. "That's right. You said you felt sure that I'd be able to slip it to you without anyone noticing."

"I don't know what you're talking about." Andy ran his finger round the inside of his shirt collar. It was getting warm. "Look, what the hell's going on?

"It's simple really." Vincent raised his eyebrows. "We all know about your little affairs." He held his hand up as Andy started to speak. "Don't bother trying to explain. And by the way." He paused and glanced over toward Don. "I'm calling in the loan. I want my money back by this Friday. Give him the letter Don."

"My pleasure." Don pulled an envelope from his inside jacket pocket. "Formal notice that the loan's being called in."

"But the agreement was for me to repay at the end of the fiscal year." Andy's faced paled. "There's no way you can call it in now."

"Read the small print, Andy." Don laughed. "Never were a man for detail were you. Always left the balls aching stuff to me. Well this time you should have been a bit more careful."

"I'll have my solicitor go through that agreement with a fine toothcomb." He knocked back the rest of the beer. "So much for a cosy lunch you're nothing but a bunch of fucking shysters. Come along Suzanne let's get out of here." He turned and started for the door.

"Hold on a minute, Andy." Suzanne moved over to stand next to Vincent. "There's some more news for you. I've had enough of your womanising." She turned to Miriam. "Sorry Miriam. I know about you and..." She nodded at Miriam. "And about Debbie and the others. Well all the bad news is coming at once. I've booked you a room at the Angel in Guildford for tonight, what you do after that is up to you but you're not coming back to the house."

"You stupid woman. At least the others were a better screw than you." His faced twisted with rage as he turned to Miriam. "Yes you were great weren't you, couldn't get enough of it. Well bollocks to the lot of you." He pointed at Suzanne. "I'll come and go in my own house as I please."

"That's another thing, Andy." Suzanne gave a shrill laugh. "The house isn't yours it's mine. And don't say it isn't because I've got the deeds at my solicitors. They're also working on our divorce. Don't try and get in I've had the locks changed and the code to the burglar alarm."

"I think you'd better go now, Clewer." Vincent moved through to the front door and opened it. "I'll be at your office at nine o'clock on Friday. A bankers draft will do. If not, don't forget your shares in the company will be mine."

"You bastard." Andy clenched his fists and moved toward Vincent. "You won't get away with this. You're trying to pull a stroke that's not legal."

Vincent stood aside from the door. "It's as legal as you getting Miriam to back a horse to lose. Now get out."

"You can write me a cheque for the rest of the money I put into your bank account, you scheming cow." Andy growled.

"What money's that, Andy? Miriam smiled. "My account my money."

"You haven't heard the last of this," He snarled as he marched through the door and climbed into his car. They heard his car start and with tyres squealing turn out of the road out of Deer Park Gardens and onto Roehampton Lane. They stood and looked at one another.

Suzanne was shaking and white faced. "I've done it." She gave a shaky smile. "I've finally stood up to him."

"I think we all need a drink, don't you." Vincent busied himself making gin and tonics. "Let's get through Friday before we start celebrating."

***

Friday came round all too quickly for Andy. The solicitor he'd shown the agreement to expressed surprise that as an astute businessman he'd agreed to such an open ended loan with such high collateral. But at the end of the day it was legally enforceable.

Vincent and Don were already in his office when he arrived at eight thirty. "Have you got the money?" Vincent was the first to speak.

"I need more time." Andy hadn't shaved that morning and you could smell last night's whisky on his breath.

"Times not on your side, Clewer." Don waved the agreement. "If you've nothing else to say we may as well wrap this up now."

"You're enjoying this aren't you?" Andy snarled. "What are you getting out of it, you slimy bastard?"

"No need for that, Clewer." Vincent leaned on the desk. "Don will become an equity share holder, something you should have done a long while ago. Would you come in please, Mr Turner."

"Who the hell are you?" Andy turned to the newcomer. "Another one of his cronies come to gloat."

"I'm Edward Turner of Snodbury and Turner, solicitors." Opening his brief case he took out a ruled legal pad and his fountain pen. "You received a formal request to repay a loan of half a million pounds as set out in this agreement." He pulled a bound copy of the agreement from the case. "Would you confirm whether or not you are going to repay the loan this morning?"

"Fuck off and go to hell." Andy snarled his face contorted with rage.

"I'll take that to mean that you are unable to pay. In that case your shares in Clewer Alternatives will be transferred to Mr Floyd and Mr Markham in accordance with the instructions I've been given and the loan agreement you signed." Edward Turner made his notes and turned to Vincent. "I think that concludes my part in this transaction. I will have my notes typed and sent to you. Where shall I send your copy Mr Clewer?"

Andy wasn't listening. All he could think of was the unthinkable. The company he'd built up was no longer his.

"Clewer, Clewer." The sharp tone of Vincent's voice brought him out of his thoughts. He looked around and saw that the solicitor had gone. "I've ordered you a taxi. I don't know where you're going but the staff here have had instructions not to let you onto the premises."

"Taxi. Why do I need a taxi I can drive myself?" His voice was full of surprise and he started toward the door.

"Just a minute." Don's voice carried an authority that Andy wasn't used to. "The cars belong to the company and you're no longer authorised or insured to drive them. The Bentley has been collected from Crondall and I'll have the keys to the Aston Martin." He held out his hand.

Thrusting his hand in his pocket Andy pulled out the keys and threw them on the floor. "I won't forget this, do you hear. I'll get even with both of you." He barged past Vincent and out of the door. The taxi was waiting in the car park and pulled away the moment he got in.

"Turner's organising for the shares to be transferred into our names. We'll have him removed as a Director of the Company. Clewer's washed up there's nothing he can do." Vincent clapped Don on the shoulder. "Well partner here's to the future." The two men smiled.

Chapter 26

A few weeks later and Andy had settled into the Angel in Guildford. It had been easier staying there than trying to find somewhere else. He'd arranged for his post to be sent on and he glanced through the letters that had been passed to him by reception.

There was one from Leisure Industries which he opened last. A pleasant surprise for a change. It was his betting account statement.

He'd forgotten that he'd also backed the horse to win. He was six thousand pounds in credit. 'Stuff you Floyd and all your pals you don't know about this.' He felt quite pleased with himself, even after he paid his hotel bill he'd have plenty of ready cash left to speculate with.

He pulled his mobile from his pocket and dialled the stables. "Adrian it's me Andy." He said when the phone was answered. "When can we run AW again?" His face fell as he listened.

"Sorry, Andy I can't take instructions from you." Adrian's voice was apologetic. "He belongs to Clewer Alternatives and they tell me you've resigned. If you're interested I got a nice eight year old for sale. He should win a race or two." He paused. "Not in AW's league of course, what do you say?"

"I'll think about, Adrian. I guess I'll see you around." He rung off and sat staring at the wall. A drink before lunch would go down well. He spotted the paper that had been delivered to his room earlier. Yes a beer or two while he picked out a couple of winners. In fact if he put a thousand pounds on the favourite in the first race at Wetherby at 6 to 4 that would give him a tidy profit of 150% straight away.

Tomorrow he thought he would go to the youth club, have a game of snooker and a chat to whoever was there. No harm in reminding them who their benefactor was.

Some of his old confidence returned, just watch out Vincent bloody Floyd, I'm on my way back!

***

Later that same day at Crondall, Suzanne was in the kitchen putting the finishing touches to a fish pie for supper when she heard car pull up and then moments later the front door opened.

"Is that you darling, supper will be about an hour, it's over the yard arm, shall I get you a drink?"

Don Markham strolled into the kitchen. "Just time for me to take you to bed. Unless you think we need more than an hour."

"We could always go back again after supper that is if you can stand the pace." Suzanne put her arms round his neck and kissed him passionately her tongue seeking his. She could feel him getting aroused. "Is it always going to be like this when you come home from the office?"

"Another new customer signed a deal with us for 25 outlets so it all depends if the deal was as good as today's." Don pressed himself against her. "Now, talking of deals why don't we go and see if we can deal with this."

About the Author

Victor Ralph is the pen name of Ian Jacombs now living in Devon with his wife Teresa having retired there some 21 years ago from the hustle and bustle of commuter life in Surrey. They are lucky enough to live by the sea with Dartmoor and beautiful countryside nearby. Gardening keeps them busy and they enjoy walking with both activities keeping them fit. Commuting nowadays is more likely a walk to the seafront and along the esplanade.

If you have enjoyed reading Alternative Ways, you might like to know that another chapter in the life of Andy Clewer is underway and will hopefully be published shortly.

Ian Jacombs
July 2024